P9-DMR-229

BINDLESTIFF

Books by Bill Pronzini

"Nameless Detective" Novels:

Bindlestiff
Casefile (collection)
Dragonfire
Scattershot
Hoodwink
Labyrinth
Twospot (with Collin Wilcox)
Blowback
Undercurrent
The Vanished
The Snatch

Other Novels:

The Gallows Land
Masques
The Cambodia File (with Jack Anderson)
Prose Bowl (with Barry N. Malzberg)
Night Screams (with Barry N. Malzberg)
Acts of Mercy (with Barry N. Malzberg)
Games
The Running of Beasts (with Barry N. Malzberg)
Snowbound
Panic!
The Stalker

Nonfiction:

Gun in Cheek

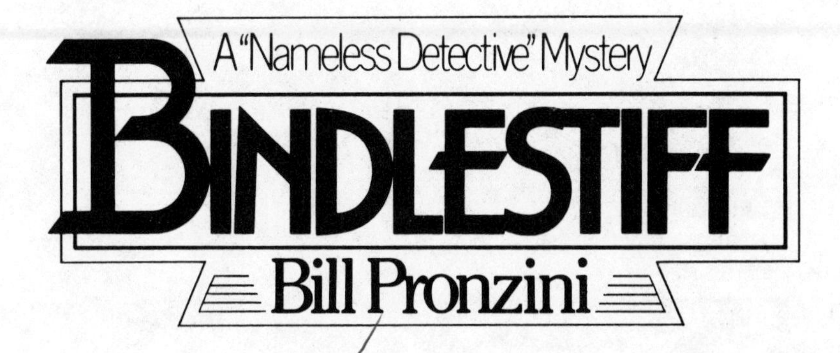

St. Martin's Press
New York

 For information, address St. Martin's Press, 175 Fifth Avenue, New York, N.Y. 10010.

Library of Congress Cataloging in Publication Data

Pronzini, Bill.
Bindlestiff : a "nameless detective" mystery.

I. Title.
PS3566.R67B5 1983 813'.54 83-9743
ISBN 0-312-07864-1

First Edition

10 9 8 7 6 5 4 3 2 1

This one is for a living legend (and an all-around good guy)—William Campbell Gault

Food we have without toil or fee,
  Nor take we heed when the tourists stare;
For every man on his grave stands he;
  And each man's grave is his own affair.

—Henry Herbert Knibbs
"Ballade of the Boes"

The hobo defies society, and [sometimes] society's watch-dogs make a living out of him . . . . It's all in the game.

—Jack London
The Road

BINDLESTIFF

1

I got my private investigator's license back on the first of October—and a job hunting for a hobo that same day.

The return of the license was far and away the more important of the two; without it I would not have got the hobo job, or any other job. That was the way it had been, in fact—no license, no livelihood—for the past two and a half months, ever since the State Board pulled my ticket for no damn good reason. Things had been so bad financially that I had had to give up my offices on Drumm Street. I had also pretty much given up hope that I would ever again work as a detective in California, the circumstances of the suspension being what they were. So getting the license back surprised the hell out of me.

But there was a catch to it. There's a catch to everything these days. In this case, the way I was put back in business and the catch were one and the same.

My old cop friend, Eberhardt.

It had been a week earlier that he'd called to give me the news. When the telephone rang I was sitting in the middle of the living room floor in my Pacific Heights flat, surrounded by pulp magazines, old newspapers, a couple of cardboard boxes, some tape and a ball of string. What I'd been doing was bundling up five hundred detective pulps, most of them from the forties and early fifties, so I could ship them off to a guy in Oregon who had paid me two dollars apiece for them. I felt lucky to get that much because they were all obscure titles—*Crack Detective, Smashing Detective, 10-Story Mystery*—and not very much in demand among collectors. I needed the money to pay my rent and buy groceries and put gas in the car so I could keep on looking for a job, any kind of reasonable job, which nobody seemed to want to give me.

Still, I hated like hell to have to let go of those pulps; it was a bad precedent. If I didn't find work pretty soon I'd have to sell another batch, and then maybe another, and before long all 6500 issues in my collection would be gone—the rare copies of *Black Mask* and *Dime Mystery* and *Doc Savage* and *The Shadow* and a dozen more titles, all gone. And then what? I'd spent better than thirty years accumulating those 6500 magazines, just as I'd spent better than thirty years working as one kind of cop or another. They were more than just a hobby; they had led me into detective work in the first place, because of my admiration for their heroes, and they represented a way of life, a code of ethics, that I had made my own. I had already had my job taken away from me; if I lost the pulps, too, what would I have left? Memories, that was all. Memories like dust motes in a patch of sunlight—and ten, twenty, even thirty more years of life without motivation.

That was what was wandering through my mind when Eberhardt called, and it was making me melancholy. I'd promised myself weeks before that I was not going to let this thing get me down any more, and for the most part, with Kerry's help—Kerry Wade, my lady—I'd managed to keep from being depressed. But some days were worse than others. This was one of the bad ones.

Without thinking, I used my left hand to push myself off the floor. Pain shot up the forearm, all the way into my shoulder. I said something obscene and flexed the fingers; most of the chronic stiffness was gone now, but the hand was still crabbed up a little and I couldn't quite use it normally yet. If I ever could. I was so preoccupied with the hand that I stumbled over one of the cartons; I cursed that, too, kicked it out of the way, and went into the bedroom and hauled up the telephone receiver and said, "Yeah?" like a dog growling at a bone.

"It's me, Eberhardt," he said. For years, his usual greeting had been something like "Hello, hot shot," but that was before the shooting six weeks ago that had landed both of us in the hospital and Eberhardt in a coma for seventeen days. And before the bribe thing that had changed his life and the simple nature of our friendship.

It was the first time we'd spoken in more than a week. I said, "How's it going? You mending okay?"

"Yeah. Getting around pretty good now. I got some news for you." And he told me about the State Board reversing itself, agreeing to reinstate my license.

I couldn't believe it at first. I said, "You're not putting me on?"

"About something like that? Hell no. You still got to go up to Sacramento for an interview, and you got to agree not to step on any more official toes in the future, but that's just a formality."

"Well, Christ, what made them change their minds? I wasn't scheduled for a review for another three and a half months . . ."

"I had a long talk with the Chief," he said. "A couple of long talks—two weeks ago, just before I got out of the hospital. I asked him to back off on you—write a letter to the Board on your behalf."

That surprised me, too; the Chief of Police had been responsible for the Board pulling my license in the first place. "And he went along with it?"

"Not at first. But I talked him into it—one last favor before my retirement. I figured he owed me that much; so did he, eventually."

"I don't know what to say, Eb."

"Don't say anything. It was the least I could do, after what happened. Hell, if it hadn't been for me you wouldn't have got shot. And you could've hung my ass out to dry on that Chinatown mess. I still don't know why you didn't. God knows, I deserved it."

"The hell with that," I said. "It's over and done with; the sooner we forget about it, the better off we'll both be."

"Yeah," he said, but he wasn't going to forget it. Not if he lived to be a hundred. I knew that and so did he. "Listen, how you doing money-wise?"

"Not so good right now, but I'll be okay. I just sold off some of my pulps."

"I thought that was going to be a last resort."

"Well, it's about that time."

"You get enough to rent another office?"

"No. But I can work out of here for the time being."

"I could spare a loan of a few hundred . . ."

"Uh-uh," I said. "We've been over that before. Thanks, but . . . no."

He was quiet for a couple of seconds. There was something he wanted to say; I could sense it. Finally he said in a low, tentative voice, "I been thinking. You know, wondering what I'm going to do with myself now that I'm off the force. I can't just sit around on my duff, even with my pension from the Department, and I'm too damn old to go into some other line of work. Being a cop is all I know how to do."

"That makes two of us."

"Yeah, well, I been thinking, like I said."

"About what?"

"About getting into your end of things. Applying for a private detective's license."

I saw it coming then. But all I said was, "It's a tough business. Hand-to-mouth."

"I know that. I got contacts, though; and a good reputation, at least as far as the public is concerned. I could drum up some work here and there."

I was silent.

"The only thing is," he said, "I don't know the ropes. I'd need somebody to point the way."

I still didn't say anything.

"Somebody like you," he said.

"Where are you getting at, Eb?"

"Ah, Jesus, you know damned well what I'm getting at. I been wondering if maybe you'd want to take me in as a partner." He went on quickly, before I could comment. "Look, I know I been a shit and I won't blame you if you tell me to go to hell. But it might work out, the two of us together. I'm a good detective; you know that. And I'm willing to let you call all the shots."

"I don't know, Eb . . ."

"I wouldn't get in your way. I mean that: you know the score and I don't. I could do legwork, promo stuff to bring in clients, anything you want."

I was silent again, because I didn't know what to say.

"You don't have to give me an answer right away," Eberhardt said. "Just think about it, will you? Will you do that?"

"All right," I said. "I'll think about it."

"Okay. Thanks." And he rang off.

So there it was: the catch. He'd called in a favor from the Chief to get my license back, and now he wanted to call in one from me and form an agency partnership. Eberhardt as a private eye? Christ.

The idea didn't set well at all. In the first place, I knew Eb. He'd said he would let me call all the shots, but he'd been able to pull rank on me for twenty years; sooner or later he'd start trying to do it again. In the second place, I had been a loner for too many years to want to take on a partner. I liked working alone, doing things my own way and at my own pace. The idea of having to share decisions and divvy up the workload wasn't too appealing. And in the third place, before the suspension I had barely made enough most weeks to pay the bills; and opening up shop again after all the hassle and publicity of the past few months was not going to be easy. Maybe Eberhardt could bring in some business, as he'd said, but there were no guarantees. Things could be lean for a long time. One man could get by on crumbs, but if you had to divide the crumbs between two men, both of them were liable to starve.

On the other hand, he *was* responsible for the State Board reversing itself. I owed him for that, and it was no small debt. If I told him no I'd be the one to feel like a shit. He would understand why I was rejecting him, but the turn-down would be there between us just the same, like a wedge. The bribe incident had already driven in one wedge, right to the point of cracking; another one was liable to split us up for good—destroy what was left of thirty-five years of friendship.

Damn, I thought. Damn! What am I going to do?

I went out into the kitchen, opened my last can of Schlitz, and took it into the living room and sat nursing it, looking at the stacks of pulps on the floor. Now, maybe, I wouldn't have to sell off any more of my collection than these five hundred issues. I should have felt more elated, more excited at that and at the prospect of getting back to work. Well, maybe it would all come sailing in on me pretty soon and I would jump up and let out a whoop or something and dance around singing "Happy Days Are Here Again." Probably not, though. Too much had happened over this crazy summer—too many complications.

My life had quit being simple during a week in June. First my relationship with Kerry, whom I'd met a few weeks previous and fallen hard for, had become strained for a variety of reasons, not the least of which was me pressuring her to get married. Then what had seemed like a business boom—three jobs in two days, all of an apparently routine nature—had degenerated into chaos: two unrelated homicides, a theft for which I'd briefly been blamed, a threatened lawsuit by one of my clients, and me stupidly and accidentally letting a murderess take it on the lam. All of this had made the papers, of course, as had my getting lucky and coming up with solutions for all three bizarre cases, so that the damned reporters had had a field day calling me "Supersleuth" and a lot of other things.

The Chief of Police hadn't liked any of that. According to him, I was making the Department look bad by upstaging his detectives. It was a public relations matter, he'd said; my acts were detrimental to the police image. Eberhardt had tried to intercede on my behalf, but he was only a lieutenant attached to Homicide, without enough cachet to make the brass listen to reason. Before long, I was out of business.

Then, as if all of that wasn't bad enough, there'd been the shooting in mid-August. I had been over at Eberhardt's house one Sunday afternoon, the two of us guzzling beer and commiserating—his wife Dana had left him for another man back in May and he'd been in a funk ever since—and the doorbell had rung, and when he went to answer it a Chinese gunman had put two slugs from a .357 Magnum into him. And one into me moments later, when I came blundering in after the shots.

Eberhardt had been critically wounded; it was a miracle he hadn't been killed outright. I'd been luckier: the bullet had taken me in the shoulder and damaged some nerves, crippling up my left arm. The police hadn't caught the gunman. They figured him for a contract slugger, but they had no idea why a contract had been put out on Eberhardt.

When I got out of the hospital I had an anonymous call from a Chinese who claimed that Eberhardt had taken a bribe, that that was what was behind the assassination attempt. I refused to believe it at first, but I was angry and I had to find out one way or the other. So I'd set out on my own investigation. It had ultimately led me to the man who'd ordered the hit; it had also led me to the truth about the bribe. And the truth was that Eberhardt had taken it, all right—or almost taken it—for looking the other way on a felony investigation.

He'd done it because he'd been despondent about Dana throwing him over; because he was getting old and tired of the long hours and the low pay and having to fight off temptation every time it reared up—all the sad, painful reasons good men sometimes commit acts that go against everything they've ever believed in. But he'd changed his mind about going through with it, then started waffling as to whether or not to change it back again. He'd still been waffling when he was shot, and he simply did not know, he said, what his final decision would have been.

We left it at that. And because I was the only other person who knew the truth—both the Chinese slugger and the man behind him had died, through no fault of mine—I left it up to Eberhardt to decide what he would do when he got out of the hospital: forget the whole thing had ever happened and go on with his police career; make a clean breast of things to the Department, face a public scandal, and probably be thrown off the force and lose his pension; or take a voluntary retirement, for personal reasons, which would allow him to keep the pension he'd earned for more than thirty years of service as a dedicated, honest cop. He had opted for voluntary retirement—probably the choice I'd have made if I had been in his position. He was now officially a civilian.

The only good thing to come out of the whole mess was that Kerry and I had got back together, and reached an understanding about our relationship, and were starting to grow closer than we'd ever been. Eberhardt and I were still friends, but there was that wedge between us, and now there might be another one.

Complications.

Nothing was simple any more. Nothing was the way it used to be . . .

I got up after a while, when I finished my beer, and went back into the bedroom and called Kerry at Bates and Carpenter, the ad agency where she worked as a copywriter. She was excited when I told her about Eberhardt getting me back into harness, but she shared my concern over the partnership thing.

"What do you think you'll do?" she asked. "Which way are you leaning?"

"You know me, babe, so you know the answer to that already. But it's going to take me a while to decide whether or not I can do it to him."

"What about *you?* Isn't what you want the important thing now?"

"I don't know yet. Maybe."

"Well, I think it is. You're not Eberhardt's keeper, you know. You didn't have anything to do with him being where he is now. And you don't owe him anything either, not any more."

"He got my license back, didn't he?"

"He also got you shot."

I sighed. "Let's not talk about that. I've been doing enough brooding about the past as it is."

"Okay. But things are finally turning around for you. Try to enjoy it, for heaven's sake."

"Will do."

"Why don't you meet me after work? We'll go out and celebrate—have dinner, maybe see a show or something. All right?"

I didn't feel much like celebrating, but I did feel like seeing her. "All right."

"Good." She paused. "Hey, you'll be a working detective again next week. That's what counts, isn't it?"

"That's what counts," I said. And it was.

So I went down to the Hall of Justice two days later and talked to the Chief of Police, at his summons, and got things more or less patched up there. Two days after that, I drove up to Sacramento and had my interview with the State Board of Licenses. They seemed satisfied that I'd "learned my lesson," as one of the Board members put it, and the vote to reinstate was unanimous; the Chief must have written them some strong letter at Eberhardt's behest. They did not even place any restrictions on me, other than to stress that I cooperate fully with all public law enforcement agencies in the future.

And on Wednesday, the first of October, I was back in business.

Hunting the hobo, for starters.

2

The fact that I landed a client that same day was not much of a surprise, really, considering there had been a fair amount of publicity attached to the reinstatement of my license. Not that I minded the publicity in this case; it was just what I needed, and I had spoken freely to the half-dozen media people who'd contacted me. Some of the news stories were good-natured and the rest were straight reportage; nobody seemed to think a menace to society or to the city's finest was being turned loose again. The consensus appeared to be, at least by implication, that an injustice had been righted and it was okay for me to be back in the detective game.

A gratifying number of people I knew, and a couple I didn't know, agreed with that. After the news stories appeared, I received maybe two dozen calls over a three-day span—six from friendly cops who hadn't agreed with the Chief's original stance; one from another private investigator, a lady named Sharon McCone whom I'd met once and who was a friend of Eberhardt's police crony, Greg Marcus; one from a claims adjustor at an insurance company and three from attorneys, all of whom I'd worked for in the past; one from a Chinese photojournalist, Jeanne Emerson, who wanted to do a feature article on my trials and tribulations; and the rest from a variety of acquaintances.

The call I'd most been waiting for, that first new client, came at a little past two o'clock. It was from a woman who identified herself as Miss Arleen Bradford. She said she'd read about me in the papers, and could I come down to her office at Denim, Inc. right away to discuss a job she wanted done. It had to do with locating a missing relative, she said. She also said she had a meeting at four o'clock, so I would need to get there by three-fifteen. I told her I would be in her office by three-ten at the latest. And I caught myself grinning a little on my way out the door.

Denim, Inc. was a clothing manufacturer—jeans and denim jackets, for the most part. Their main offices were located in an old brick building on Mission Street, on the fringe of the Hispanic district. It was just three when I parked in the front lot, five past when I got up to the fourth floor, and not quite ten past when one of a battery of secretaries ushered me through a door that bore the lettering: A. BRADFORD, PRODUCT MANAGER.

Arleen Bradford turned out to be a thin, wiry, prim-looking type in her mid-thirties. She might have been attractive if she'd put on about fifteen pounds, done something to her dark brown hair other than have it cut with a bowl and a pair of hedge clippers, and worn something besides a mannish gray suit and a blouse with so many frills and ruffles on the front that you couldn't tell whether or not she had breasts. As it was, she looked like an uneasy combination of successful modern businesswoman and budding old maid. She sounded and acted that way, too. On the phone she had been crisp and businesslike, but she had also made a point of referring to herself as *Miss* Arleen Bradford, not Ms.

She gave me a brief appraising look, and her eyes said I was about what she'd expected a detective to be: one of those big, hairy brutes with dubious ethics and not many morals. She let me have her hand for about half a second and then took it away again as if she were afraid I might do something unnatural with it. She didn't have a smile for me, and I didn't have one for her, either.

"Thank you for being so prompt," she said. "I have a meeting at four, as I told you."

"Yes, ma'am."

"Please sit down."

I sat in a plain chair with gray-frieze cushions. Judging from the surroundings, "product manager" was a title that carried relatively little weight in the company. The office wasn't much, just a twelve-by-twelve cubicle containing her desk, two chairs, a filing cabinet, and a window that looked out over Mission Street.

From one corner of the desk she picked up a newspaper folded into thirds and handed it to me without speaking. Then she went around and sat down. I looked at the paper. It was a copy of the *Examiner,* the afternoon tabloid, and it was folded open to a story on page three that was headlined: THE NEW GENERATION OF HOBOES. There was also a photograph of four men gathered around an open fire in a field; in the background, you could see railroad tracks and what appeared to be a freight yard.

I started to skim the story. It was one of those human interest features you see more and more of these days, about people who have fallen on economic hard times. Specifically, in this case, about out-of-work men who ride the rails from one place to another looking for menial jobs—

men otherwise known as hoboes, tramps, vagabonds, bindlestiffs, knights of the open road. That sort of individual was supposed to be an anachronism, the story said, that had pretty much disappeared with the end of the Great Depression. But with unemployment at its highest rate since the thirties, and government cutbacks in a variety of job programs, there was a whole new generation of bindlestiffs out there riding the rods, sleeping in boxcars or in hobo jungles, eating mulligan stew and canned pork and beans, drinking cheap wine to chase away the cold and, sometimes, to keep their sad and painful memories at bay. The bunch of hoboes pictured were stopovers in Oroville, up in Butte County, one hundred and fifty miles northeast of San Francisco, where the Western Pacific Railroad had a switching station and freight yards. They had come off a cannonball freight from Los Angeles and were waiting to board another freight bound for Pasco, Washington, where they would pick fruit—

"The man on the far left is my father," Arleen Bradford said.

I glanced up. "Pardon?"

"In the photograph," she said in a flat voice, as if she were confessing some sort of unpleasant family secret. "My father, Charles Bradford."

I studied the photo. The quality of reproduction was pretty good; you could see the faces of the four men clearly. The one on the far left was around my age, early to mid-fifties, with a gaunt, beard-stubbled face bisected by a thin blade of a nose. He wore a perforated summer cap with a wide visor, and an old work shirt open down the front. Around his neck was something that looked like a pendant, elliptical in shape and hanging from a thin chain.

"Are you sure it's your father?" I asked her.

"Of course I'm sure. I haven't seen him in three years, and he's changed quite a lot, but there's no mistake. Besides, he's wearing the pendant I made for him when I was in high school." Her mouth quirked bitterly. "Daddy never cared much for me, but he was always fond of that silly pendant. I can't imagine why."

I didn't want to get into that sort of thing with her, unless it was relevant to the job she was hiring me to do. "You want me to find your father, is that it?"

"Yes."

"Why? If it's to convince him to give up the hobo life, I'm afraid that's not in my—"

"What he does with his life is his own business," she said. Her voice was full of cold disapproval, like a spinster schoolteacher discussing a wayward child. "I want you to find him and deliver a message, that's all."

"What sort of message?"

"That he contact me immediately, regarding his Uncle Kenneth's estate."

"I don't understand, Miss Bradford."

"His uncle died ten months ago," she said. "No one in the family thought Uncle Kenneth had any money, but it turned out that he did—all in stocks and bonds. Hardly a fortune, but enough to make several bequests. One to me, one to my sister Hannah, and one to my father, among others: twenty thousand dollars to each of us. The attorneys handling the estate made every effort to locate Daddy at the time the will was probated, but they were unsuccessful."

"When was it that he dropped out of sight?"

"A year and a half ago, not long after he lost his job with the Office of Minority Business Enterprise."

"That's a Federal agency, isn't it?"

"Yes. And a productive one before that idiot in Washington started his massive cutbacks. My father had been with the Los Angeles branch of OMBE for eighteen years—he worked in Procurement, obtaining construction contracts for minority firms—but this administration has no respect for minorities or for individuals. He was given a month's notice and thrown out on the street."

"Did he try to find another job?"

"Of course. The last time I spoke with him on the telephone, just before he . . . went away, he said he'd been jobhunting almost daily. But he wasn't qualified for anything except bureaucratic work, and he has no particular skills. No one would hire him."

I knew all about that. And all about the state of the economy and the high rate of unemployment. Nobody had been willing to hire me during the past two and a half months either. But I said, "Why would he have decided to become a hobo? I mean, he could have taken on menial jobs without traveling around in boxcars. Riding the rails isn't the kind of thing you expect of an ex-government bureaucrat."

"No, it isn't. It's degrading and disgusting, and I think he's a fool." She sounded a little angry now, as if she'd taken the fact that he was hoboing as a personal insult. "But that's neither here nor there. I suppose he did it because he considers the life of a tramp adventurous."

"How do you mean?"

"He has always been fascinated by trains," she said. "And by hoboes, God knows why. His favorite book was that dreadful thing of Jack London's, *The Road*. He collected books on trains, and he belonged to a model railroad club in Los Angeles. Our flat was always full of tracks and miniature cars and grown men wearing engineer's caps. Pure nonsense."

"Mmm."

"He's a fool," she said.

Maybe he is, I thought, but you're a pip yourself, lady. I said, "If you don't mind my asking, why are you going through the expense of locating him?"

"I beg your pardon?"

"You don't seem to like your father very much, and you consider him a fool. Why pay a detective to hunt for him so he can claim his inheritance?"

"He is entitled to the money," she said stiffly. "My

sister may not care if he gets it, but I do; I know my duty."

"Why doesn't your sister care?"

"Because she doesn't care about anyone except herself. She never has. Besides, she's greedy."

"Greedy?"

"There is a stipulation in Uncle Kenneth's will that if any of us were to die before the estate cleared probate, or if any of us fails to claim his bequest within two years, that person's share is to be divided among the remaining two. Hannah would like nothing better than to get her hands on another ten thousand dollars."

"She's not very well off, is that it?"

Miss Bradford's mouth turned bitter again. "No, that's not it," she said. "Hannah doesn't have to worry about money. Her late husband left her a house in Sonoma—her *third* husband, and she's only thirty-three. She ran off to Nebraska with some man when she was eighteen, left him and married a rock musician, and then left *him* and married Joe Peterson, a man older than Daddy. And now she's engaged to be married again, to a well-to-do businessman. Thrills and money, those are the only things she's ever been interested in."

"I see," I said. And I did see; Arleen Bradford disliked her sister a hell of a lot more than she disliked her father. Sibling rivalry, maybe. Or maybe she just didn't like anybody very much.

"That twenty thousand dollars belongs to my father," she said. "I intend to see that *he* gets it."

"It might get expensive, you know," I said, "my tracking him down. That photo was taken sometime yesterday, and the article says he was on his way to Washington to pick fruit; he'll probably be long gone by the time I can get to Oroville. If that's the case, I'd have to go on up to Washington myself . . ."

"Do whatever is necessary to find him," she said. "Within reason, naturally. I'll expect regular telephone reports and an itemized list of your expenses."

Uh-huh, I thought. I decided not to do any more pursuing of her motives. Whatever kind of screwy love-hate feelings she had toward her old man, and however she felt about her sister, it was really none of my business. She wanted a job done, and I was back in the profession; that was the bottom line. The fact that I didn't like her worth a damn had nothing to do with it either.

I said, "All right, Miss Bradford. It's a little late for me to accomplish much today; I'll leave for Oroville first thing in the morning. And I'll call you as soon as I have anything to report."

She nodded. And then got out her checkbook, without my having to ask for a retainer, and wrote out a check for a hundred dollars. I took it in exchange for her signature on one of my standard contract forms. She read the contract twice before she signed it; I would have been surprised if she hadn't.

Then she said, "Now if you'll excuse me, it's almost time for my appointment. I'll expect a call from you or my father sometime tomorrow. If it's after business hours, I'm sure I'll be home; my home number is on the check." And that was all: I was dismissed. She didn't get up, she didn't offer me her hand again, she didn't even look at me as I stood and went over to the door and let myself out.

Some daughter, I thought on my way to the elevator. Fifteen minutes with Arleen Bradford made me feel relieved that I had never married and had kids of my own.

But I was still in pretty good spirits. Even the likes of Miss A. Bradford hadn't been able to put a damper on them.

God, it was good to be working again!

3

It was four–thirty when I got back to my flat. I had taken the telephone answering machine out of the box of stuff I'd brought home when I gave up my office, and hooked it up here, and I checked that first thing. There was one message, another call from Jeanne Emerson. Would I ring her back as soon as it was convenient?

I frowned a little, thinking about her. This was the fourth or fifth time she'd called over the past six weeks—a persistent young lady. An attractive young lady, too; I remembered the long, glossy black hair that hung like a curtain down the small of her back, the perfect oval of her face, the olive-black eyes that slanted only a little. One of the most attractive Oriental women I had ever seen, in fact. I might have been interested in her if it hadn't been for Kerry—not that she would have been interested in *me* that way. As it was, Kerry would have been upset if she'd known the sort of male fantasy I was indulging in just then.

I got a beer out of the refrigerator, took it back into the bedroom, and dialed Jeanne Emerson's number. She answered right away. After I told her who was calling I said, "You don't give up, do you?"

"No," she said, "I don't. I intend to keep pestering you until you agree to let me do that feature."

"I'm not that interesting a subject, believe me."

"I think you are. You represent the common man's struggle to maintain his ideals while working within a restrictive system."

"Hah," I said.

"No, I mean it. You've overcome terrific odds; you're still in there fighting. You're a throwback to a different era, when people cared about others and heroes were important. That's what you are—a full-fledged hero."

She was making me feel self-conscious. I was no hero;

I screwed up too much and had too many problems to be one. And I was no selfless saint either. Those were lofty standards I could never live up to.

I said, "If that's the sort of article you want to do, I guess you'd better find somebody else. I'm just not your man."

"But you are. You're exactly the man I want." There was something in her voice, a faint inflection, that hinted at more than an impersonal, professional meaning to that. Or was I just imagining it? "Besides, it would be good publicity for you."

"Well . . . how would you do the article?"

"As an intimate personal portrait; the fact that you're a detective would almost be secondary. Emphasis on your pulp collection and how it relates to your way of life. It really could be good, you know."

I had seen some of her photographic work; it probably would be very good. "Where would you publish it?"

"That depends. I have an editor friend who works for *California* magazine; he might be interested. That would give you a lot more exposure than if it's published locally."

"Uh-huh. When would you want to start?"

"Right away. Whenever you're free."

"I've got to go out of town tomorrow," I said; "I picked up my first new client this afternoon. I don't know how long I'll be gone."

"Why don't you call me when you get back? Or do you want me to call you next week sometime?"

"I'll call you, I guess. And give you a definite answer then."

"Fine."

We said good-bye, and I put the receiver down. That damn fantasy ran around inside my head again. Some selfless saint. Jeanne Emerson wanted to tell the world how noble I was, and all I could think about was what it would be like to go to bed with her.

Well, it was harmless speculation. Even if she *was*

interested in me personally, which I didn't believe for a minute, I had no intention of pursuing things with her. Maybe I would consent to letting her do the article, but that was as far as it would go. I was in love with Kerry; I would be a fool to do anything to jeopardize my relationship with her, now that we had something solid together. The last thing I needed was another complication in my life.

I started out of the bedroom—and the telephone rang again behind me. I thought it might be Kerry, because we had a date for dinner and she hadn't been sure what time she would be through with work; but when I picked up the receiver, an unfamiliar woman's voice said my name and asked if I was the private investigator.

I said I was, and she said, "My name is Hannah Peterson. I understand my sister hired you this afternoon."

"If your sister is Arleen Bradford, she did."

"Yes. Well, I wonder if I could stop by and talk to you about that? I'm in the city now, downtown; I could be at your place in about fifteen minutes. That is, if the address in the phone book is correct."

"It is. What did you want to talk about, Mrs. Peterson?"

"Couldn't I tell you in person? It would be so much easier."

I remembered what Arleen Bradford had told me about her sister. If that verbal portrait was reasonably accurate, I was probably not going to like much whatever it was Hannah Peterson had to say to me. But then, I was inclined to take anything Miss A. Bradford had to say about anybody with several grains of salt. It wouldn't hurt to talk to Mrs. Peterson, find out what was on her mind.

"Come ahead, then," I said.

"Thanks a lot. I'll be there as soon as I can."

I cradled the receiver and went into the living room. Usually the place was a mess; I was something of a slob when it came to housekeeping. But now that I was going to be working out of the flat for a while, until I had enough money in reserve to afford new offices, I had cleaned up the place and resolved to keep it that way. It looked pretty good. I had even dusted the shelves flanking the bay window, where nearly all of my six thousand remaining pulps were displayed.

My arm was starting to bother me a little; it hurt sometimes in the afternoon and early evening. It stiffened up just from using it in normal activity—particularly if I was out in cool or cold weather. The therapist I'd been going to the past three weeks had given me a set of exercises to do when that happened. I had other exercises to do, too, to strengthen the damaged motor nerve. The chances were good, she said, that in time I would regain full use of the hand—"less than two percent impairment," was the way she put it—and have only occasional stiffness. She was very upbeat about the whole thing, one of these cheerful optimists; on good days she bolstered my spirits and on bad days she depressed me. You pays your money and you takes your chances. I'd know for sure which way it was going to go in another few months.

So I went through the series of exercises, went through them a second time. The hand and arm felt better when I was done, and so did I. I went out into the kitchen and made myself a cup of coffee. I was just starting to drink it, using my left hand to grip the handle, when Hannah Peterson showed up.

In answer to her ring I went and buzzed her in downstairs, then opened the apartment door and waited for her to climb the stairs. I don't know what I expected her to be like—a slightly more appealing version of Arleen Bradford, maybe—but she was some surprise. Honey-blond hair, sloe eyes, one of those pouty Marilyn Monroe mouths painted the shade we used to call shocking pink; tall, svelte, with good hips and better breasts encased in a white pants suit that had gold threads woven through it. But there was nothing of the dumb blonde about her. If anything, she was street-wise; the sloe eyes were shrewd and calculating, and just a little hard, and when she put them on me it was like being slapped and caressed at the same time. A ballbuster, I thought. The kind who went through men like a bad wind, leaving a wreckage of broken hearts and broken spirits in her wake. No wonder Arleen Bradford hated her and probably hated men, too. There wasn't a straight male on this earth who would look twice at prim little Arleen when fast Hannah was around.

She gave me her hand and a sultry smile, smacked me again with those eyes. She was after something, all right, and it wasn't me. But what she didn't know was that I was on to her. And that I found Kerry—and Jeanne Emerson, too, for that matter—a hell of a lot more exciting than I could ever find her. Blond hair and big boobs have never done much to melt my chocolate bar, as the Hollywood folks say.

So I took the hand, let go of it again, made my own smile impersonal, said, "Pleased to meet you, Mrs. Peterson. Come in, won't you?" and backed away from her.

The heat coming out of her eyes cooled a little as she stepped inside; she seemed momentarily nonplussed, as if she couldn't understand why I was not responding to her. I turned away from her to shut the door. When I turned back again the bewilderment in her expression was gone: she thought she had me pegged now. The smile changed shape and became a sly sort of smirk. She said, "Thank you again for letting me stop by," and the tone of her voice was different, too, with the sex bleached out of it—a kind of just-between-us-girls intimacy.

For Christ's sake, I thought, she thinks I'm gay!

It struck me funny and I almost laughed out loud. San Francisco has the largest, most outspoken and well-publicized homosexual population in the country; a lot of people who don't live here, who only come to the city occasionally or not at all, seem to think just about every other male or female is of the lavender persuasion. I hadn't reacted to Hannah Peterson the way she expected, ergo I must prefer boys. It was ridiculous—but the world is full of ridiculous people.

I managed to keep a straight face, so to speak, and decided not to say anything to alter her misconception. Let her think I wore lace panties and kept a male harem; what the hell. If she knew the truth she would only turn the sex on again. And I did not want to have to deal with that.

I said, "Sit down, Mrs. Peterson. I've got some coffee in the kitchen if you'd like a cup."

"No thanks. I won't stay long." She sat on the couch, crossed her legs, and got a pack of cigarettes out of her purse. "Do you mind if I smoke?"

"Go right ahead."

She lit up, letting her eyes wander around the room as she exhaled smoke. "You have a nice apartment," she said. "It's so, um, masculine."

I said, because I couldn't resist, "An interior decorator friend of mine designed it."

"He's very good."

"Yeah," I said. "He's a sweetie."

"All those old detective magazines are a nice touch. Do you actually read things like that?"

"Oh no, they're just for decoration . . . because I'm a private eye myself. But I'm going to get rid of them one of these days; they collect dust."

"I imagine they must."

"Besides, they're full of stories about murder and violence and human fiends doing all sorts of disgusting things to women. Detective work isn't really like that, you know."

A faint frown line appeared on her forehead, as if she might be tumbling to the fact that I was putting her on; but then it smoothed away and she nodded seriously. She may not have been a dumb blonde, but she sure as hell was a credulous one.

But the joke had gone far enough; this was supposed to be a professional discussion. I said, "What was it you wanted to talk to me about, Mrs. Peterson?"

"My father. That photograph of him in the paper and my sister hiring you to find him."

"You saw the photograph, did you?"

"Yes. I came into the city to do some shopping—I live in Sonoma—and I stopped for a drink afterward at the St. Francis. There was a copy of the *Examiner* in the lounge. Well, I called Arleen right away, and she told me she'd hired you to go up to Oroville and look for Dad."

"And?"

"I think she made a mistake. I'm here because I'd like you to reconsider doing what she wants."

"You mean you don't want your father found?"

"*He* doesn't want to be found," she said.

"Oh? How do you know that?"

"He told me as much himself. The last time I talked to him, before he went off to ride the rails."

"I don't think I understand."

"You have to know Dad. Up until he lost his job with the government, he led a very uneventful life. I guess Arleen told you he's always been fascinated by trains and by the hobo life. Well, losing his job gave him the chance to go ahead and do what he'd always dreamed about doing."

"Being a hobo," I said.

"Yes. Spending the rest of his life around trains. He doesn't really care about money, you see. Not at all. Uncle Kenneth's twenty thousand dollars wouldn't matter to him if he knew about it; he'd go right on being a hobo."

"He's still entitled to it."

"But he wouldn't bother to claim it, that's the point. He'd want Arleen and me to have it."

"Your sister doesn't seem to think so," I said.

"Of course not." She punched out her cigarette in the coffee-table ashtray. "Arleen . . . well, Arleen is strait-laced; she thinks she knows what's best for everybody. She's always tried to run my life and Dad's. Frankly, he was fed up with her. That's one of the two reasons he told me, and not Arleen, when he decided to go on the road."

"What's the other reason?"

"He knew I'd understand because I've always loved trains, too—anything to do with trains. I guess his interest in them rubbed off on me when I was a kid."

"Have you had any contact with him over the past year and a half?"

"No. He wanted it that way."

"Doesn't that bother you?"

"Not really. We've never been close; closer than he and Arleen, but not tight. Anyhow, even if you went to Oroville and found him, he wouldn't call her any more than he would try to claim his inheritance. He doesn't want anything more to do with Arleen. He only wants to be left alone."

"That ought to be his decision to make, don't you think?"

"But he's already made it," she said. She sounded faintly exasperated, as if she were trying to get an obvious point across to somebody who wasn't very bright. "He told me he never wanted to see or hear from Arleen again. It would only upset him if you found him and told him about Arleen seeing his photograph in the paper and hiring you. It wouldn't do any of us any good."

"Except maybe your sister."

"Oh, damn my sister. She's a frump and she's made Dad's life, and mine, miserable for years. You met her; can't you see what kind of person she is?"

I had seen that, all right. And I saw what kind of person Hannah Peterson was, too. Five would get you ten she cared a hell of a lot less about her father than she cared about her half of the twenty-thousand-dollar bequest. And that she harbored the same deep-seated sibling hatred as Arleen had for her. They were quite a pair, these two. Maybe Charles Bradford *would* be better off if I didn't find him and try to toss him back into the clutches of his offspring.

But that was not my decision to make. And I found it difficult to believe that Bradford would want Arleen and Hannah to have his twenty thousand dollars; he'd probably want to claim the money even if he never used it, just to keep them from getting their claws on it.

I said, "All of that may be true, Mrs. Peterson, but I don't see that I can turn down the job just because you want me to."

Her nostrils pinched up; she was starting to get angry. "If it's the money I'll pay you whatever amount Arleen is giving you—"

"It's not the money," I said. "If I go along with your wishes, what's to stop your sister from hiring another detective?"

"You could always tell her you went to Oroville and you couldn't find Dad. That would satisfy her."

I shook my head. "I'm sorry, I can't do it. I've already agreed to the job; it's a matter of professional ethics—"

"Professional ethics!" she said, as if they were a couple of four-letter words. "I read about *you* in the paper, too. I know what kind you are."

"You do, huh? I don't think so, lady."

"You bet I do." She got to her feet, glaring at me; it was the kind of look that could cut a hole in a piece of steel. She was on the verge of throwing a tantrum. "You're just like my sister—a nasty little piece of work who won't listen to reason. I hope they take your license away again. I hope you go straight to hell."

I stood up too. "Good-bye, Mrs. Peterson."

"You damned *fag!*" she said, and stormed over to the door and went out and slammed it shut behind her, hard enough to shake the pulps on their shelves.

I sat down again. I was angry myself, but it didn't last long. What was there to be angry about, after all? Hannah Peterson was a spoiled and greedy thirty-three-year-old sex object, and I had just stuck a pin in her balloon and deflated her. Score one for the side of manipulated males everywhere.

Then I thought: You damned *fag,* you—and burst out laughing.

4

"She actually thought you were gay?" Kerry said. She seemed to think that was the most comical thing she'd ever heard; there were tears of mirth in her eyes. "Lord, I wish I'd been there to see it!"

"It was some session, all right," I said.

"It must have been." She wiped her eyes on her napkin, and then put one elbow on the table and cupped her chin in her hand and gave me her oh-you're-such-a-delightful-man look. "There's never a dull moment in your life when you're working, is there? First you take a job to go chasing after a hobo, then you have a run-in with a sex bomb who thinks you're gay. Wow."

I couldn't tell whether or not she was putting *me* on. She had an off-the-wall sense of humor, and I suspected that she took a great deal of satisfaction in keeping me off balance whenever she could. Sometimes she made me feel awkward and confused, sometimes she made me angry, and sometimes she made me feel like a jerk. But none of that did anything to change my attitude toward her. She was so damned attractive it made me ache a little just to look at her: shiny auburn hair, wide mouth, green eyes that changed color according to her mood, and a body—as Raymond Chandler once wrote—to make a bishop kick a hole in a stained-glass window. She was also intelligent and mostly fun to be with, and I loved her like crazy.

Jeanne Emerson? I thought. Hannah Peterson? Give me Kerry Wade any old time.

It was a little after seven o'clock and we were sitting in a cozy Japanese restaurant on Irving Street, near the University of California Medical Center, having *sashimi* and chicken *yasai* and cups of hot sake. And I had just finished telling her all about my day: Arleen Bradford, my imminent trip to Oroville, and Hannah Peterson. Other diners were looking at us because of Kerry's outburst of laughter—not that I cared much.

I said, "It's still a pretty routine job. If I get lucky and Bradford is still in Oroville, I'll be back home tomorrow night."

"Maybe so. But you've got to admit, it does have its unusual elements."

"That's for sure."

"You know," she said, "I'll bet he really is enjoying himself."

"Who? Bradford?"

"Yes."

"I'm not so sure. The man's down-and-out. And being a hobo is a hell of a road to have to travel, once you get started on it."

"Oh, I don't know. Hoboing has its romantic aspects. Besides . . . 'Every man on his grave stands he, and each man's grave is his own affair.'"

"Huh?"

"Two lines from a poem about hoboes I read once. They just popped into my mind."

"Pretty profound stuff," I said. "But I still say it's a hell of a road to have to travel."

"You don't think it can be adventurous?"

"Not as far as I'm concerned."

"You mean you've never wanted to ride the rails, just once, to see what it was like?"

"No."

"Well, suppose you have to go up to Washington to find Bradford. How will you travel?"

"Drive, I guess."

"It'd be faster by train," she said. "You could always hop a freight and pass yourself off as one of the tramps."

"Is that supposed to be funny?"

"No, I'm serious. That's what I'd do if I were you. Just for the experience."

"That kind of experience I don't need."

"Why not?"

"I'm too old for it, for one thing."

"You're not any older than Charles Bradford."

I had a mental image of myself huddled in the corner of a dusty boxcar, staring out at a lot of dark, empty terrain, listening to the rhythm of the wheels and the locomotive's whistle echoing in the night. It wasn't a very pleasant image. It made me feel cold.

"No thanks," I said. "The closest I intend to get to a freight train is the Oroville hobo jungle. And the sooner I get out of there, the better I'll like it."

A lock of her auburn hair had fallen over one eye, giving her a vaguely sultry look, like a redheaded Lauren Bacall. She brushed it away and took a thoughtful bite of her chicken *yasai.* "What's a hobo jungle like, anyway?" she asked. "I've never been anywhere near one."

"Good. They're not very pretty. And not very safe either. Not everybody who beds down in them is one of your romantic vagabond types."

"No?"

"No. Fugitives ride the rails, too—thieves, murderers, you name it. And toughs, jackrollers."

"What's a jackroller?"

"Somebody who rolls drunks or tramps for their money, and isn't afraid to use violence when he does it."

"Really? Well, you'd better be careful when you go running around up there."

"Don't worry, I will."

She nodded, then looked thoughtful again. Pretty soon she said, "You know, I think my mother wrote a story about a hobo jungle once. In fact, I'm sure she did. It was published in *Clues.*"

Kerry's mother, Cybil, was a former pulp writer, and a very good one; surprisingly, she had written some of the best hard-boiled detective stories to appear in the forties, under the male pseudonym of Samuel Leatherman. Ivan Wade, Kerry's father, was also a former pulp writer, but he had specialized in horror fiction. I liked Cybil and hated Ivan the Terrible, primarily because he thought I was too old for Kerry—I would be fifty-four my next birthday and she would be thirty-nine—and was always after her to break off our relationship.

I said, "Do you remember the title of Cybil's story?"

"Not offhand. I . . . wait, yes I do. It was one of those dumb titles they used to put on pulp detective stories, 'The Case of the Stiff Bindlestiff.'"

"Ouch," I said.

"Pretty bad, all right. But it was a good story; it had to do with some sort of smuggling activity involving tramps and trains."

"I'll look it up when I get home. Was it one of her Max Ruffe stories?"

"I think it was."

Max Ruffe was Cybil's best pulp character, a tough, cynical, but still human private eye. Not all of her Ruffe capers were first-rate, because pulp writers had had to turn out reams of copy in order to make a living and couldn't afford to spend much time rewriting or polishing, but the best of them put her in a league with Chandler and Hammett and the other big guns.

We ate in companionable silence for a time. Then Kerry said, "Have you thought any more about what you're going to do about Eberhardt?"

"Some."

"Still no decision?"

"Not yet. It's such a damned no-win situation, no matter which way I go."

"No-win for whom? Not for you, not if you tell him no."

"Not as far as business is concerned, maybe. But I've got a feeling it would put an end to our friendship."

"If it does it's his fault, not yours."

"I'm not so sure about that."

"Does his friendship really mean that much to you? After all that's happened?"

"Come on," I said, "you know the answer to that. I don't have many close friends; and I'm not the kind to give one up just because he made a mistake. Besides, Eberhardt needs all the support he can get right now."

Kerry nodded; she understood. "If you decide that you do have to take him in with you," she said, "couldn't you do it on a trial basis? Three months or so, to see how it works out?"

"I thought of that. But I don't think he'd go for it. It would look like I'm testing him."

"Well, what if you take him in and it doesn't work out? You'd have to dissolve the partnership to protect yourself. And that would probably end the friendship anyway."

"I know. But at least I'd have tried. And maybe it *would* work out. You never know for sure until you try."

"You don't really believe that."

"No," I said. "We're different people, Eb and me; we don't look at life or the detective business the same way. The reason we've got along so well all these years is that we've only seen each other two or three times a month, only worked together occasionally since I left the force. Put us together on a daily basis, his way of doing things would clash with mine. We'd probably wind up at each other's throats."

"Then the best thing to do is to say no right now. Don't put either of you through it."

"So I keep telling myself. The problem is, I can't seem to get up enough gumption to go through with it."

There was nothing more to say on the subject, not now, and we let it drop. Any further discussion would only have depressed me and I did not want to spoil the evening for either of us.

We drank a pot of tea and had *katsetura,* a Japanese sponge cake, for dessert. When we left the restaurant we went for a leisurely drive through Golden Gate Park, out past Sea Cliff and up into the Presidio to where you could look out over Baker Beach and the Golden Gate Bridge and the entrance to the Bay. It was a nice night, clear except for scattered wisps of cloud, and we lingered up there until well after dark. By the time I drove back crosstown and stopped the car in front of Kerry's apartment building on Diamond Heights, it was after ten o'clock.

"I think I'd better say good night right here," I said. "I want to get an early start for Oroville in the morning."

"Poor baby. You're tired, huh?"

"A little."

"Just want to go home and crawl into bed."

"Yeah."

"Alone."

"Yeah."

"And go right to sleep?"

"Maybe I'll read a little first . . ."

"Cybil's story about the stiff bindlestiff?"

"If I have that issue of *Clues.*"

"Clues," she said. "You detectives are always after clues of one kind or another."

"If you say so."

"Well, I'll tell you something. There are clues and then there are clues. And you never know where you might find them. There are clues right *here,* for instance."

"Right where?"

"Right here in this car, right now."

"What kind of clues?"

"The kind that'll lead you to a body, if you pick up on them."

"Whose body?"

"Mine," she said. "Come on up for a few minutes, detective. See if you can find the body."

"Well," I said, weakening, "I guess I could do that. But just for a few minutes."

"Sure. Just for a few minutes."

So I went upstairs with her, and found the body all right, and it was a few *hours* before I got out again, long past midnight. I didn't do any hunting for *Clues* when I got home to my flat; I was too tired to turn on the damn light.

5

Oroville was a small town with a permanent population of around ten thousand, set up against the foothills of the Sierra Nevada at the western edge of the Mother Lode. It had been built on an ancient river bed so rich in gold that a dredging outfit had once offered to buy and move every one of its buildings in order to mine the ground. Mining had been its principal industry from the days of the Gold Rush through the early 1900s. Then thousands of acres of olive, nut, and a variety of fruit trees had been planted in the surrounding area, and canning and packing companies moved in, and the Western Pacific established its freight yards on the outskirts. That brought in a substantial number of itinerant fruit pickers, a good many of whom were hoboes catching free rides on the freights that passed through.

And then, in 1967, the state of California had completed construction of the huge Oroville Dam on the Feather River that wound down through the town. This had created Oroville Lake a few miles to the north, which was popular with boaters, fishermen, and family day-trippers. During the warm-weather months, the itinerant fruit pickers were joined by droves of tourists; and summer-home and retirement communities had sprouted and flourished like weeds in the vicinity of the dam.

The town itself hadn't changed much, though. If anything, it seemed to be deteriorating. It was quiet and tree-shaded, but the last time I had passed through, a little over a year ago on a fishing trip to the north fork of the Feather River, the old downtown area had had a neglected look and many of the homes were run-down. Recently there had been some trouble with a neo-Nazi faction in the area, which may or may not have had something to do with the fact that not many people were on the streets. Most of those who were out were grouped at the small shopping centers and fast-food places along Oro Dam Boulevard, the main through road. The overall feeling of the place was a little depressing.

I pulled into Oroville a few minutes before eleven on Thursday morning, after a nonstop, two-and-a-half-hour drive east to Sacramento and then north on Highway 70 through Marysville. It was hot up there, muggy, with a high cloud cover that gave the sky an unpleasant milky cast and the sun the look of a cataracted eye. The weather, the sky, and that leaden aura made me hope I would be on my way out of here again pretty soon.

I stopped at a Mobil station on Oro Dam Boulevard for gas and directions to the Western Pacific yards. They weren't far away; I made a right-hand turn on Lincoln two blocks up and drove less than a mile before the freight yards appeared off on my right.

Ahead, a side road branched in that direction and paralleled the yards. On this side of the fork was a corrugated-iron building, painted a sort of mustard yellow and set back off the road behind a wide gravel lot; a sign in front proclaimed it to be the Guiding Light Rescue Mission. The article in yesterday's *Examiner* had said that Oroville's main hobo jungle was located near the mission.

I swung onto the side road. On the left, facing the Western Pacific facility, were several blocks of near-slum houses whose only redeeming features seemed to be an abundance of trees and other vegetation that softened their squalid lines; at least some of them, I thought, would belong to past and present railroad workers. The yards stretched out for a good fifth of a mile—an intricate network of tracks and sidings, a long roundhouse, corrugated-iron sheds, repair stalls, water and fuel tanks, overhead strings of sodium vapor lights, and switch engines and out-of-service boxcars, flats, tankers, and refrigerator cars. Near the entrance was a trailer that I took to be the yardmaster's office. Beyond to the southwest were empty fields of dry brown grass, with bunched-up sections of rocky hillocks, thick underbrush, and wilted-looking live oaks and conifers. Somewhere over there, hidden by hummocks and brush, was the hobo jungle.

The road petered out a short way past the entrance to the yards, at a gate that barred access to a main line of tracks. I turned around and drove back to the fork and parked on the side of the road next to a dusty field. I walked across the field, then crossed another line of tracks to a shallow ditch. It was hot and still over here. You could hear faint noises coming from the freight yards; there weren't any trains running at the moment. When I looked over the terrain to the east, to where the distant forested slopes of the Sierra loomed up dark and indistinct, the glare of the sun coming through that milky haze was almost blinding.

Crossing the ditch, I went up through thirty yards of barren earth strewn with rocks. A path had been worn through the dry brown grass beyond, angling upward over one of the hummocks; I moved along there. I still didn't see or hear anybody—not until I was halfway across the top of the hummock. Then, a short distance away on my left, where the terrain flattened out again and there were the remains of several campfires, I spotted a man standing in front of a scrub pine.

At first I couldn't tell what he was doing; but as I moved closer, I realized he was shaving. There was a broken piece of mirror attached to the tree by a piece of string, and he was peering into it as he scraped at his face with a straight razor. He wasn't using any lather. Just the razor and some water from a tin can he held in his other hand.

I walked up on one side of him, slowly, so that he could see me coming in the mirror. But he didn't turn. And he didn't quit scraping the razor over his cheek. He was a big guy, with not much hair and a roll of fat on his neck that bulged over the collar of a faded blue T-shirt. He looked about forty.

Five paces from him I stopped and said, "Morning. Mind if I talk to you for a minute?"

No answer. He dipped the razor blade into the tin can, shook the water and beard stubble off it, and went right on shaving.

"Excuse me," I said, a little louder. "I'd like to talk to you."

Still no answer. The scrape of the blade was audible in the stillness.

"Look, mister," I said, "I know you can see me in that mirror. Are you deaf or what?"

He took the razor away from his face, dunked it in the can again, shook it—and then, in unhurried movements, he pivoted in my direction. His eyes had a bloody look, and there was something a little wild about them; they stared right through me.

"Fuck off, 'bo," he said.

The words came out quiet, without any heat, but they were thick with menace just the same. The skin along my back tightened. I didn't like those eyes, and I didn't like the way he was holding that razor. He was nobody to prod; he was nobody I wanted to deal with at all.

I said, "Sure, 'bo," in the same kind of voice he'd used, and took a couple of steps away from him to my right. He didn't move, watching me. I put my back to him, a little tensely, and went past a couple of the cold campfires to where the path cut between some shrubs. Nothing happened. I made myself walk without looking back until I came up onto another piece of high ground. When I turned my head he was facing the mirror again, working the razor over his chin—just a fellow having himself a quiet morning shave.

A short distance ahead I came to another clearing. This one was occupied by two men sprawled in the shade of a live oak. One of them was leaning against a propped-up backpack, the kind campers use, and the other was lying with his head pillowed on a bedroll.

The one leaning against the backpack saw me first; he said something to the other man, and they both got to their feet in wary movements. I hesitated before I approached them, feeling just as wary. But they didn't look particularly dangerous, and I did not see any potential weapons; I went ahead. They were standing shoulder to shoulder when I reached them, watching me with eyes that were neither friendly nor unfriendly. A couple of more or less harmless tramps, these two. As long as nobody did anything to rile them up.

"Howdy, gents," I said. "You been around here long, have you?"

They were still sizing me up. Even though I was wearing an old pair of slacks and a chambray work shirt—you didn't go mucking about in a hobo jungle dressed in a suit and tie—they knew I wasn't one of their fraternity.

"What's it to you?" the taller of the two said, finally.

"I'm trying to find a man who was here two days ago. Hobo named Charles Bradford, on his way to Washington to pick apples."

"Yeah?"

"His daughter's trying to locate him. For family reasons." I dug out the photograph I had clipped from the *Examiner* and passed it over. "Bradford's the man on the far left."

The two tramps studied the photo. "Don't know him," the tall one said. "You, Hank?"

"No," Hank said.

"We just rolled in this morning, mister. Headed south. You better talk to one of the residenters."

"You mean hoboes who live here permanently?"

"Yeah. Over that way." He pointed to the southeast. "There's a gully. You'll find it."

"Thanks."

"I'd walk in careful if I was you. They don't take much to outsiders."

"I'll do that."

He gave the clipping back to me, and I went off to the southeast through tall grass that was so dry it crunched like eggshells underfoot. The gully was a good three hundred yards away—shallow, wide, with underbrush and scrub pine growing along both banks. Clustered at the bottom were half a dozen one-room shacks made out of wooden frames and tar paper, a couple of them with corrugated-iron roofs; some had badly hung doors, some had nothing more than a flap of heavy tar paper across their entrances, and none had glass windows. I didn't see any power lines; they probably didn't have running water, either.

There was a communal fireplace in the center of the little complex, and sitting around it on rickety chairs that had no doubt come out of a trash dump were three old men—bindlestiffs who had retired because of old age or health reasons, but who wanted to live out their lives near the railroad. They had been passing around a near-empty gallon jug of white port wine, but they quit doing that when they saw me.

I made my way down a narrow path into the gully, my shoes sliding on the loose earth. None of the three men got up and none of them moved; they just sat there, stiff and staring, like blocks of gnarled old wood. They were all in their late sixties or early seventies, and one of them, the biggest and maybe the youngest, was black. Like the previous two tramps I'd talked to, their expressions were guardedly neutral.

I pulled up about ten feet from them. "Sorry to bother you," I said, "but I could use some help. I'm looking for—"

"Help's something we're fresh out of," the black man said. He had white hair and a grizzled white beard, and he must have weighed in at two hundred and fifty pounds, not much of it fat. The thumb on his left hand was missing. "Try the mission. They got lots of it, so they say."

"Sympathy, too," one of the white guys said. "Plenty of help and plenty of sympathy."

"Sympathy, hell," the other white guy said. "You know where you find sympathy? In the dictionary between shit and syphillis."

All three of them laughed. Then they quit laughing

and looked at me, and the black one said, "This here's private property, man. You trespassing."

I reached into my back pocket, being careful about it so they didn't get any wrong ideas about what I was going for, and took out my wallet. Inside I found a ten-dollar bill and held it up where they could see it. Then I nodded toward the gallon jug the black guy was holding on his lap.

"You're almost out of wine," I said. "Hot day like this, a man gets pretty thirsty."

None of them said anything, but they were watching the money.

"Ten bucks buys a cold jug for each of you," I said.

They stirred, exchanged quick looks. The black man asked, "What else you figure it buys?"

"A little information, that's all. I'm looking for a hobo named Charles Bradford. He came through here two days ago on his way north and managed to get his picture taken." I put my wallet away and held up the newspaper clipping.

"Them San Francisco reporters," the first white guy said. He was over seventy, thin and wizened, and he had a crippled-up look about him, the way people suffering from acute arthritis do. "We wouldn't talk to 'em."

"Well, Bradford talked to them," I said. "And if he's still around I need to talk to him."

"Cop," the second white man said. There was so much ground-in dirt on his seamed face that he looked sooty, as if he'd been caught in the middle of a recent fire.

I sensed that if I admitted my profession it would close them off; hoboes didn't like cops, and it did not matter if they were public, private, or the railroad variety. I said, "No, I'm not a cop."

"I know a cop when I see one."

"Do cops offer to buy you a jug of wine?"

"He got you there, Woody," the black guy said. He seemed to have relaxed a little. He asked me, "What you want with this Bradford?"

I told him the same thing I'd told the other tramps. Then I went over to where he sat and extended the clipping.

He took it, but he didn't look at it. "The ten bucks first," he said.

"Do I get straight answers?"

"We hoboes, man, not grifters. You get what you pay for."

I let him have the money. He put it away in the pocket of his dirty gray shirt and then gave his attention to the photograph. "Which one's Bradford?"

"The one on the far left."

He studied the photo some more. When he was finished he passed it on to the white guy named Woody, who squinted at it myopically for about five seconds before he handed it to the third tramp.

I said, "Well? Do any of you know him?"

"Seen him around," the black man said. "They call him 'G-Man'—used to work for the gov'ment."

I nodded. "Do you know if he's still here?"

"No. Ain't seen him since the reporters come around."

"He's the one got in the hassle with the streamliner," Woody said. He glanced at the other white guy. "You remember, Flint. Kid that come off the freight from Sacramento."

"Yeah," Flint said. "Long-haired little bastard. I remember."

I said, "What are 'streamliners'?"

"Young dudes, mostly," the black guy said, "not real tramps. They travel without a bedroll, only the clothes they got on they backs. Dopers, most of 'em; this one was for sure. Runnin' from something or somebody. Or just plain runnin'."

"And Bradford had some trouble with one?"

"I seen it myself," Woody said. "Just after them Frisco reporters left. This streamliner come off and tried to mooch some stew G-Man was cooking up."

"What happened?"

"They had them a little push-and-shove. Then the streamliner, he pulled a knife. Couple of the other 'boes run him off before he could do any cuttin'."

"Was that all there was to it?"

"No," Flint said. "Kid went over into the yards and come back a while later. I seen him."

"I seen him too," Woody said. "So did G–Man. Three of us was there together. G–Man had him some Cadillac and he didn't mind sharing it."

"'Cadillac'?"

Woody grinned; what teeth he had were decayed stumps. But it was the black guy who answered my question. "Bottle of Thunderbird," he said. "Cadillac of tramp wine."

"Did anything happen when the streamliner showed up the second time?"

"He didn't know we seen him," Flint said. "He was headin' for the road with a signal lantern in one hand and a tool kit in the other. Swiped 'em from one of the sheds."

"Prob'ly on his way into town to try sellin' the stuff for the price of dope," the black tramp said. He shook his head. "Damn long-hairs give hoboes a bad name. Yard bulls hassle all of us because of 'em."

"Just what I says to G–Man," Woody agreed. "And he says something ought to be done about it and by God, he was goin' to. I told him why don't he mind his own business, but he wouldn't listen. Reckon he was still thinkin' about the streamliner tryin' to cut him with that knife."

"You mean he chased after the kid?"

Woody wagged his head. "Nope. Says he's goin' to report what the long-hair done; tell the yardmaster or one of the bulls. He went off into the yards. Left the Cadillac with Flint and me. Nice fella, G–Man."

"What time was that?"

"I dunno. Three o'clock, maybe."

"Did you see him again?"

"Nope."

"How about the kid?"

"Nope."

"Freight come through since then bound for Pasco?"

"Yesterday morning," Flint said.

"So Bradford—G–Man—could have hopped it."

"Could have, but he didn't. Me and Woody and Toledo was all over there when she pulled in; we seen the tramps that got aboard. G–Man wasn't one of 'em."

"There been any other northbound freight?"

"Nope," the black man, Toledo, said. "Next one's due tomorrow morning."

I considered that. Then I asked, "The streamliner happen to mention his name?"

"Not that I heard," Flint said, and Woody wagged his head again.

"What did he look like?"

"Long hair like all of 'em got. Yellow. Scrawny little bugger; couldn't of weighed more than a hundred and thirty stripped."

"What was he wearing?"

"Levi's. No shirt, just one of them sheepskin vests—"

In the distance there was the wailing blast of a locomotive's air horn. The three old tramps stirred immediately and came to their feet as one. Toledo said to me, "That be the noon southbound out of Medford. She comin' in to change crews."

They started away from me toward the path that led up the gully wall. Trains were their lives, and with one coming in—and my ten dollars' worth of information just about used up anyway—they had lost interest in me. Flint, the one with the arthritis, had trouble making it up the slope. Toledo hoisted him under one brawny arm, the way you'd pick up a child, and carried him to the top.

I went up after them. The Medford freight was just clattering into view from the west—a string of maybe thirty cars, most of them boxes and flats. The air horn shattered the hot morning stillness again.

The three hoboes headed into the yards, toward the siding the freight was shuttling onto. I followed them, but it wasn't the freight I was interested in. The person I wanted to talk to now was Western Pacific's day yardmaster.

6

I found the yardmaster in his office, in the trailer I had noticed earlier near the entrance to the yards. His name was Coleman and he was about sixty, lean and sinewy, wearing an orange hard hat even though he was sitting at his desk. I was honest with him about who I was and what I was doing there; he seemed willing to cooperate. The only problem was, he had nothing to tell me.

"No," he said when he was done looking at the newspaper photograph, "I've never seen this man before."

"But you *were* here around three o'clock on Tuesday afternoon?"

"I was. Out by the freight storage shed, as I recall, discussing a shipment of wheel flanges with a local businessman. Nobody who looked like this fellow Bradford came to see me."

"Well, maybe he talked to one of the yard security men . . ."

Coleman shook his head. "If he had, it would have

been reported to me. Theft is a serious offense around here and we damned well don't put up with it. We did miss a signal lantern and a tool kit two days ago; the lock on one of the sheds was forced. But no one owned up to seeing the man who stole them or I'd sure know about it." He paused. "Who did you say told you about this?"

"Three oldtimers who live over in the hobo jungle," I said. "Woody, Flint, and Toledo."

"Well, they've been around a long time and there's not much goes on that they don't know about. They're as reliable as tramps can be." Coleman shrugged. "Maybe Bradford changed his mind about reporting the theft. Hoboes don't want to get involved, as a rule."

"Yeah," I said. "Maybe he did."

I left the trailer and went back across the yards and the open field to where I had parked my car. I didn't know what to think now. If Bradford had changed his mind about reporting the streamliner, where had he gone instead? And why hadn't he hopped the freight for Pasco, as the newspaper article said he'd planned to do?

I wondered if he might have stopped by the rescue mission. That seemed as good a bet as any, so I drove back there and into the gravel lot. Off to one side of the mustard-yellow building were a couple of gardening sheds and a vegetable patch; drawn up in front was a battered old pickup truck. There was no sign of anybody in the vicinity. And when I got out and went up to the front door I found it locked; a hand-lettered sign taped to it said BACK AT 2:30.

What now? I thought as I returned to the car. I decided to try canvassing the houses that faced the rail yards, on the chance that one of the residents had seen Bradford on Tuesday and maybe had some knowledge of where he'd gone. I spent an hour doing that, but it got me nothing except a lot of blank looks and doors slammed in my face.

Was it possible Bradford had gone into town and taken a flop for the night? It didn't seem likely. But he might still have gone into Oroville for some other reason—and so might the streamliner with his stolen loot; I remembered Toledo saying that the kid had probably done that to sell the stuff for the price of dope. I still had no proof that there was any connection between Bradford's apparent disappearance and the streamliner, or that the two of them had had any further contact, but it was an angle worth checking out.

I drove back to Oro Dam Boulevard and then took Myers Street downtown. Oroville wasn't a very big place; the downtown area was maybe a dozen square blocks of old buildings, some with turn-of-the-century false fronts, and narrow sidewalks that didn't have many people on them. The part of it that catered to transients and local down-and-outers was a couple of sleazy blocks along Montgomery and Huntoon streets, near the river—and near a green cinder-block structure that housed the Oroville Police Department. It was almost as if the cops had established themselves close by in order to keep an eye on the town's unsavory elements.

It occurred to me when I saw the police station that maybe Bradford had been arrested as a vagrant. Hoboes were always being rousted by cops in small railroad towns, particularly if they wandered in among the local gentry. If Bradford had been picked up he might have missed his northbound freight yesterday because he was in jail. I drove up to the green cinder-block building, parked the car in a slot facing the river, and went inside to find out.

The officer at the desk was a young, flat-faced sergeant with straw-colored hair who gave his name as Huddleston. You have to be careful in how you deal with small-town cops; some of them don't like private detectives from the big city—a sort of professional hostility, because they think you're there to stir up trouble on their turf. But Huddleston wasn't like that. He was polite, if a little reserved, and when I showed him the photostat of my license his face registered nothing more than mild curiosity.

"What can I do for you?" he asked.

"I'm looking for a man named Charles Bradford," I said, and spread the *Examiner* photo on the desk in front of him. "He's the man wearing the perforated cap."

"Yes, I saw this in the paper the other day," Huddleston said. "Pretty good story, as these things go. Why are you looking for this Bradford?"

I explained it to him, briefly but without leaving out anything pertinent. I also told him about the streamliner and the rest of what I'd learned at the hobo jungle. "I thought maybe you might have picked Bradford up on a vag charge."

He shook his head. "Can't help you there. We've only booked one man in the past couple of days—drunk and disorderly—and he isn't Bradford."

So much for that idea. "I don't suppose it was the kid, either?"

"Nope. Local fellow; railroad worker who likes his booze too much and picks fights when he's in the bag."

"Well, I guess I'll just have to keep poking around. That is, if you have no objections."

"None as far as I'm concerned. We're interested in this streamliner, though; we don't like thieves in Oroville. Or dopers. If you turn up a lead on him I'd appreciate you letting us know right away."

"Sure thing. Thanks for your time, sergeant."

"Good luck."

I went outside, looked at my car, decided to leave it where it was for the time being, and walked across Montgomery Street. I still had my original idea to check out—that either Bradford or the kid, or both of them, had come into town on Tuesday and ended up down here in the transient area. Even if neither of them was here now, somebody might remember having seen one or the other.

There were two pawnshops, both on Huntoon Street. The guy who ran the first one had never seen either the streamliner or Charles Bradford, or so he said; but the proprietor of the second place admitted that yes, a young longhair had come in on Tuesday afternoon, late, and tried to hock a railroad lantern and a box of tools.

"But I sent him packing," the pawnbroker said. "Tramps bring stuff they steal from the WP yards in here sometimes. I don't have nothing to do with 'em."

"If you figured the stuff was stolen, why didn't you report it to the police?"

His mouth got tight at the corners. "I didn't *know* it was stolen. Hell, I got a business to run here. I can't be calling the police every time somebody comes in with something they want to hock."

Uh-huh, I thought. "Do you know any place where the kid might have been able to unload the lantern and tools? Someone who's not as honest as you are?"

"No," he said flatly. "There ain't nobody like that in Oroville."

He was lying; there's someone like that in every town of this size, and especially a town with the transient population of Oroville. Maybe he didn't want to confide in me because I was a stranger, or maybe he just didn't want to get involved. In any case, he was firm about it so there was no point in pressing him.

The block of Montgomery Street north of Huntoon was jammed with cheap hotels, cafés, bars, and gambling clubs advertising low-ball and draw poker. I started at the near end and worked my way along, giving the newspaper photo and a description of the streamliner to bartenders, waitresses, desk clerks, cardplayers, and bunches of elderly men with vacant eyes and liquor on their breaths. A third of them wouldn't talk to me, and I didn't trust half of the rest to give me a straight answer. Nobody knew Bradford, nobody knew the streamliner. Nobody knew anything.

I had pretty much given up by the time I walked into the Miners' Hotel—ROOMS BY DAY, WEEK, OR MONTH—near the end of the block. The lobby was small, gloomy, smelled of dust and disinfectant, and had some faded plush furniture that hadn't been new at the time of the 1906 earthquake; a guy about ninety with a nicotine-stained white mustache was half buried in one of the chairs, unmoving, as if he'd died there and been stuffed as some sort of monument. Behind the desk, a middle-aged rheumy type in an undershirt was watching a soap opera on television. He looked like a character out of a 1930s detective pulp; all that was missing was a green eyeshade and a pair of suspenders.

Nothing happened in his expression when I showed him the photograph, but when I described the streamliner an immediate flicker of recognition came into his eyes. Then the eyes got crafty. He smelled the prospect of money; you could almost see his nose twitch.

"Well," he said, "I dunno. I might know that one. Then again, my memory ain't what it used to be . . ." He shrugged and watched me, licking his lips.

There was no percentage in playing games with him. If I told him I was a cop he'd ask to see my badge. And if I told him I was a private detective he'd still want to get paid. So I took a five-dollar bill out of my wallet, laid it on the counter with my hand on it and enough of the numeral showing so he could see it, and said, "How do you know him? Did he come in here?"

"That's right," the clerk said. "Now I remember." He wasn't looking at me anymore. His eyes were all over the money; I could feel them like crawling things on the back of my hand. "Fella looked like that come in Tuesday evening and took a room."

"Was he alone?"

"Yeah. Alone."

"What name did he register under?"

The clerk did not have to consult his book. "Smith," he said. "Mr. Smith, from Sacramento."

"Did he just stay the night, or what?"

"No. Paid two nights in advance."

"Then he hasn't checked out yet?"

"Far as I know, he's still up in his room. Far as I know, he ain't been down since he registered."

"What room is he in?"

"Six. Second floor, rear."

"I'm going up for a little talk with Mr. Smith," I said. "But you don't know that. So you can't call up and let him know I'm coming, now can you?"

"I don't know nothing," the clerk said. "I told you, mister, my memory ain't what it used to be."

I took my hand off the fiver and moved toward the stairs at the rear. I didn't see him snatch up the bill, but I heard him do it and I heard him smack his lips. It was like listening to a carrion bird swoop down on the carcass of a small animal.

7

The second-floor hallway was dim and quiet and had the same dust-and-disinfectant smell of the lobby. The first door I came to was standing open, and when I passed it I glanced inside automatically, the way you do. A frowsy brunette in her middle thirties was sitting on the end of the bed, clad in an old Hawaiian muu-muu. One foot was propped against a chair, so that the muu-muu bunched up to reveal a lot of flabby white thigh; she was painting her toenails blood-red.

She saw me and paused, and she must have hopped up immediately as I passed. I had only taken a half dozen more strides along the hallway when I heard her call behind me, "Hey there, sugar," in a voice that sounded as if it had been marinating in a vat of bourbon. When I turned she was leaning against the door jamb, one hand resting on an outthrust hip; the pose was as old as time, and so was the smile on her bright red mouth. "What's your hurry?"

"I'm here on business," I said.

She laughed. "That makes two of us, sugar. Come on in when you're through and we'll get acquainted."

"I don't have the time. Thanks anyway."

"Special rate for big guys like you."

"Uh-uh. Sorry."

I pivoted away and went on down the hall, looking at the numerals on the closed doors. When I got to the one with 6 on it I moved up close and put my ear against the panel. There wasn't anything to hear. I rapped on the wood and called out, "Mr. Smith?"

No answer.

I knocked again, waited through another fifteen seconds of silence, then reached down and tried the knob. Locked—what else? "Mr. Smith? You in there?"

"He's in there, all right," the pudgy hooker said. She hadn't gone back inside her room; she was still leaning back there against the jamb, watching me. "But he ain't gonna open the door."

"No? Why is that?"

She came down to where I was, making a little production out of it, like a stripper coming down a burlesque-house runway. "How come you want him?" she asked in an undertone. "Don't tell me you're the Man?"

"The Man" was what street people called a pusher, a dealer in drugs. "No," I said.

"I didn't think so. You ain't a cop either; I can spot a cop with my eyes shut."

Sure you can, honey, I thought. She was so good at spotting cops, she probably had an arrest record as long as a bad novel.

"So what do you want with that grubby little shit in there?" she asked. "If his name is Smith, mine's Bo Derek."

"It's a private matter."

"Yeah, sure. Well, he ain't gonna answer the door, like I said. But if you want to get in there and wake him up I can help you out."

"How?"

"The door locks in this fleabag are all the same. You got a key to one room, you got a key to all of 'em."

"Is that so?"

"Yep. You can use my key, sugar."

"How much?"

"Ten bucks." She grinned and stroked her hip suggestively. "Put another twenty with it and you can use me too."

Everybody had a hand out these days; money was everything, money was life itself, and nobody seemed to much give a damn how he got it. The "Screw-'em-all-except-me" philosophy was becoming universal. These were hard times, all right. If you didn't watch out for your own ass, nobody else was going to do it for you.

I got a sawbuck out of my wallet, waggled it in front of her nose, and said cynically, "The key, sugar. Just the key."

"You don't know what you're missing," she said, and I thought: The hell I don't. But she turned back toward her room, disappeared inside for a few seconds, reappeared carrying the key. I let her have the ten in exchange for it, slid the key into the latch, turned it until the tumbler clicked, and then withdrew it and gave it back to her.

"So long," I said. "Have a nice day."

"You too, sugar."

She returned to her room, jiggling her fleshy hips to let me see again what she thought I was missing. I waited until she went inside and shut the door; then I faced number six. And rotated the knob and shoved the door inward, cautiously, hanging back on the balls of my feet just in case.

But I didn't think there was going to be any trouble—and there wasn't. He was sprawled on his back on the bed, a skinny kid of about twenty-five with sallow skin, a concave chest, pipestem legs, and filthy yellow hair that lay in long matted ropes over the pillow. Even though he was conscious and his eyes were staring straight at me, he didn't know I was there. He didn't know he was there either: he was about as stoned as you can get. Little giggles came out of him like invisible bubbles out of one of those kids' soap toys. The room was hot and sticky and foul with the sweet-acid smell of marijuana.

I shut the door, breathing shallowly through my mouth, and went over to a window that looked out on an airshaft and opened it to let in some fresh air. Then I moved over by the bed. The ashtray on the nightstand was full of roach butts, and there were two fresh joints in an empty can of Prince Albert tobacco. The way it looked, he'd managed to sell the stolen lantern and tools, scored a load of grass from one of the local suppliers, and come here to do some solo flying; that would explain why he hadn't left the room for two days, why he'd paid for both days in advance.

But judging from the number of butts in the ashtray, and how stoned he was, he'd been smoking something stronger than plain grass. Marijuana soaked in angel dust, probably, I thought. Angel dust was a chemical compound called PCP, an animal tranquilizer, and it was not very expensive. What it *was* was dangerous. People had suffered brain damage and any number of other side-effects from taking it.

That didn't stop dopers like this one from using it, though, because it was supposed to give you a terrific high. They were the new lost generation, these kids, drifting from one place to another, looking for something they'd never find in a hazy half-world of drugs and dreams. Highs were all that mattered to them; escape from a reality they feared or hated or were bewildered by. Only they never got high enough, because there wasn't anything on this earth that could elevate them to where they wanted to be. And sooner or later, if they didn't get help or wise up on their own, they would take a trip—real or drug-induced—that they wouldn't come back from.

The kid wasn't wearing anything except a pair of dirty shorts; his pants were on the floor, along with his sheepskin vest and a pair of heavy motorcycle boots. I picked up the pants, found a wallet in one of the back pockets. There was no money in it, but it did contain a California driver's license with his picture on it. He had to carry the ID in case the police rousted him, because without it he'd be arrested on the spot. The license said that his name was Stanley McGhan and that once upon a time he had lived in El Cajon, down by San Diego.

I put the wallet away, sat on the edge of the bed, and slapped him open-handed across the face. He didn't move and he didn't stop giggling. I swatted him again, and kept on swatting him, rhythmically, back and forth, back and forth, until my arm got tired and his face glowed a fiery red. The giggles quit first, after about five minutes; then he stirred, tossed his head around on the pillow; and finally he began to come out of it.

As soon as his eyes focused on me, and enough of his memory came back for him to remember where he was, he started to struggle. I said, "Take it easy, Stanley," and slapped him again. Fear danced on his face; he tried to lunge off the bed. But the drugs still had control of his motor responses, so that he might have been trying to fight his way up through water. It was pathetic, and it made me feel angry—at him for screwing up his life, and at myself for sitting here and pounding on him like some sort of surrogate father.

I slapped him another time, threw him back flat on the bed and pinned him with my weight. "Listen to me, Stanley," I said. "I'm not a cop and I'm not here after your dope. You understand?"

I had to repeat it twice more before it registered. He quit struggling then and his mouth opened and closed a couple of times like a beached trout's. "Who're you, man?" he said. "What you doin' in my room?"

"I'm looking for the man you had a fight with at the hobo jungle. Right after you came off the freight from Sacramento on Tuesday."

He heard me, all right; and his eyes were clear enough, so that he understood what I was saying. But his face twisted up as if the words made no sense to him, as if he thought he might still be hallucinating.

"Thin guy," I said, "middle fifties, wearing a charm on a chain around his neck. You wanted some of the food he was cooking and he wouldn't give it to you, so you pulled a blade on him. Remember?"

He remembered; you could see the relief come into his expression, because it was something that did make sense and it meant he had a grasp on sanity again. But it was fear I was looking for and the fear was gone. The memory of Charles Bradford held no terror for him, seemed to hold nothing at all for him except confusion.

"Yeah," he said. "Yeah."

"Did you see him again after the fight? Talk to him again at the hobo jungle or here in town?"

"No. What's goin' on? What . . .?"

"Think hard, Stanley," I said. "When I leave here you don't want me to come back. You don't want me to smack you any more. Right?"

"Right. Yeah."

"Did you see him again after the fight?"

"No. I told you, man, no!"

He was telling the truth, I thought. He had to be; he was still too stoned to pull off a convincing lie. I let go of him and straightened off the bed. He lay there without moving, staring up at me, his face still full of confusion. Anguish, too: he was sliding back into the real world again, where there was hassle and pain, and he didn't like that. He didn't like it at all.

I looked at him a couple of seconds longer, trying to make up my mind what to do about him. But then he made a noise in his throat, halfway between a sob and another of those giggles, and rolled over and pawed the Prince Albert can off the nightstand. That made up my mind for me. I did not owe Stanley McGhan a damned thing; I owed myself and I owed the law, and that was all. I was on my way out the door when he shoved one of the remaining joints into his mouth and struck a match with trembling hands to light it.

The pudgy hooker's door was open again; I went on past it this time without looking inside. Downstairs, I used a public phone to call Sergeant Huddleston at the police station and told him where he could find his thief. That solved his problem for him; and that of Coleman, the yardmaster at Western Pacific. But I was still left with mine, and it was as puzzling as ever.

What had happened to Charles Bradford?

8

I stopped for a sandwich and a cup of coffee at a café on Myers Street, and it was after three o'clock when I drove into the gravel lot fronting the Guiding Light Rescue Mission. A white van with the name of the mission printed on its side was parked next to the pickup now. And the front door of the building stood open.

I pulled in next to the van, got out, and entered a big common room, with benches along one side and some folding chairs and a dais on the other. No religious trappings except for a cross and a bronze sculpture of the Virgin Mary on the wall behind the dais. The room was deserted, but after a couple of seconds a giant of a guy materialized through a door at the far end and approached me.

He was at least six-five and three hundred pounds, and he had a dark red beard and enormous hands; his size, the plaid shirt and corduroy trousers he wore, and the beard gave him the appearance of a lumberjack. But when he got up close you could see the missionary look—the mixture of compassion and piousness—in his eyes.

"Good afternoon," he said. "May I help you?"

"I hope so. Are you the proprietor?"

"I am. J.L. Baxter. The J.L. stands for Jerome Leon; my parents were fine people, but . . ." He shrugged and smiled quizzically at me.

I explained who I was and why I was there, then pointed out Bradford in the newspaper photo. "Have you ever seen this man before?"

"As a matter of fact," he said, "I have. I spoke to him a couple of days ago."

"Do you remember what time that was?"

"Late afternoon. Around four."

"Did he come here to the mission?"

"Not exactly. I was out working in my vegetable garden and he was walking across the field from the freight yards. When he saw me he detoured over." Baxter smiled again, a little sadly this time. "I thought he might want shelter or a hot meal, but he only wanted to ask me a question."

"Do you mind telling me what that question was?"

"Not at all. He wanted to know where the library was."

"The library?"

"It surprised me, too," Baxter said. "A library is not the sort of institution hoboes are generally interested in."

"Did he say why he wanted to go to the library?"

"No. And I didn't ask."

"Did he say anything else?"

"No, nothing," Baxter said. "He seemed a bit preoccupied and in a hurry, and he went off again as soon as I gave him directions."

"How do you mean, preoccupied?"

"Oh, very much self-involved at the moment. As if he was excited about something."

"You haven't seen him since then, by any chance?"

"No."

I described Stanley McGhan, but Baxter had never set eyes on anyone who looked like the streamliner; he'd only been working in his vegetable garden a few minutes when Bradford came by, he said. So he'd probably been inside when the kid passed with his stolen goods.

I asked Baxter how to get to the library, thanked him for his time, listened to him wish me luck, and then went back out to my car. Now what the hell? I was thinking. Up to this point, everything had added up: Bradford's fight with McGhan, the kid's theft of the lantern and tool box, Bradford and a couple of retired tramps seeing Stanley make his getaway, Bradford deciding to be public-spirited and report the theft and then going off into the yards—all a logical sequence of events. But then it all seemed to go haywire. Bradford hadn't talked to the yardmaster or any of the yard bulls; instead, he'd come hurrying back past the mission a little while later, excited about something and apparently on his way to the public library. Something must have happened in the yards to shift gears for him. But what? And what could a hobo possibly want at the library?

Well, maybe somebody there could give me some answers. I started the car and went to find out.

The library wasn't far away, less than a mile from the mission on Lincoln two blocks east of Oro Dam Boulevard. It was a low, newish, beige-and-brown building with the words BUTTE COUNTY LIBRARY in big raised letters on the front wall. There were only three other cars in the parking lot; Oroville's hall of learning, it seemed, wasn't exactly a popular hangout for the residents.

The checkout desk, L-shaped and made of blond wood, was just inside the front door. Behind it, a thin young guy with a nose like a boat hook was pasting card pockets into a stack of recent acquisitions. The only patrons I saw were an old guy sitting at one of the tables, shuffling through a stack of magazines, and a studious-looking kid browsing in the section marked NEW ARRIVALS—7-DAY BOOKS.

I told the thin guy behind the desk what I wanted and started to show him the *Examiner* photo, but he said he hadn't been on duty Tuesday afternoon; the person I wanted to see was Mrs. Kennedy, the head librarian. She was there, doing something over in the stacks, and he went and got her for me.

Mrs. Kennedy was about sixty, silver-haired, energetic, and garrulous. She peered at the photo through a pair of reading glasses and said immediately, "Oh yes, I remember him. Frankly, I was amazed when he came in. I mean, I could see that he was a tramp—the way he was dressed and the pack he was carrying and all."

"Yes, ma'am."

"They just don't come in here. I mean, the library is the *last* place you'd expect to find a hobo."

"Yes, ma'am," I said. "Do you know what it was he was looking for?"

"Well, that amazed me even more. I was at the desk and he stopped and the first thing he asked was if we keep microfilm files of old newspapers."

"Old newspapers?"

"Yes. Well, I told him that we do, and he asked if the *Los Angeles Times* was one of them."

"Is it?"

"Oh yes. Most libraries keep microfilms of at least one major daily newspaper, you know, and the *Los Angeles Times* is the standard one in small branches such as ours. We also have files of the *San Francisco Chronicle* and the *New York—*"

"Yes, ma'am. Did he ask to see the *Times* files?"

"He did. The ones for the months of August and September of 1967."

I ruminated about that for a couple of seconds. Screwier and screwier, I thought. "Did he give you any indication of what he wanted from those files?"

"No, he didn't," she said. "He studied them for twenty minutes or so, in our microfilm room. That was all."

Twenty minutes was hardly enough time to wade through two months' worth of issues of a thick daily newspaper. That being the case, it would seem that Bradford had to have known more or less what he was looking for.

"You said those files were the first thing he asked about," I said. "Was there something else he was interested in seeing?"

Mrs. Kennedy nodded. "The Oroville city directories for the past fifteen years. He spent another few minutes with those. Isn't that strange?"

"It is," I agreed. "Very. I don't suppose he told you why he wanted to look at the directories?"

"I'm afraid not."

"Did he ask for anything else?"

"No. As soon as he was finished with the directories, he practically ran out of the building. He almost knocked me down and he didn't even bother to apologize. Well, I was speechless, I really was."

I didn't believe that for a minute. "Did you happen to see which direction he went?"

"No, I didn't," Mrs. Kennedy said. "I was too perplexed to pay any attention."

I considered asking her for those same microfilm files of the L.A. *Times* for August and September 1967. But without more information, some clue as to what Bradford had been looking for, it would be like hunting the proverbial needle in a haystack. The same was true of the Oroville city directories. My best bet was to try to trace Bradford's movements after he'd left the library.

He'd been on foot, and as far as I knew he wasn't familiar with the layout of Oroville. If he'd been heading for some place here in town, as his study of the directories seemed to indicate, he might not have realized until after he'd rushed out that he needed directions to wherever it was. And he might have stopped somewhere else to ask how to get there.

I went to see if I could get there myself.

9

I made an arbitrary decision and turned west out of the library parking lot, toward the downtown area. There were a bunch of industrial establishments, and a couple of restaurants along Lincoln Boulevard in that direction; I wasted forty minutes asking questions and showing the newspaper photo to a dozen people. Nobody had seen Bradford on Tuesday or on any other day. Nobody seemed to give much of a damn about hoboes either.

So I turned around finally and drove back toward Oro Dam Boulevard, past the library to the east. A middle-aged attendant at a service station on the main drag allowed as how he might have seen a guy who looked like Bradford walking by on Tuesday afternoon; he always noticed tramps, he said, because sometimes they came in and tried to mooch a handout. But he'd been busy at the time and he couldn't be sure it was the same guy in the photograph.

There was another service station across the street; I drove in there and talked to a fat kid with pimples who said he'd also been on the job on Tuesday afternoon. "I think I seen him," the kid said. "He started in here like he wanted to ask me something, but I was waiting on a customer. So he went on out again."

"Do you remember which direction he headed?"

"North. Yeah, toward the dam."

In the next block there were a couple of fast-food places, an auto supply store, a music store, and a combination grocery and liquor retailer. I drew a blank at all of them. But on the corner of the next block after that, I came on a place called the Green Garden Café—a small lunchroom with a lot of potted plants in the window and a bunch more decorating the long, narrow room inside.

There was nobody in the café when I entered except for a fairly good-looking bleached-blond waitress in her twenties and a burly guy about the same age wearing the uniform of a deliveryman, with his shirt sleeves rolled up so you could see that his arms were covered with tattoos. The two of them were down at the other end of the counter, facing each other across it. The waitress was grinning all over her face and watching the burly guy expectantly. Neither of them seemed to notice I had come in.

"Here's another one," the guy was saying. "You'll

love this one, Lynn. How come the Italians don't have a national fish?"

"How come?"

"They did," he said, "but it drowned."

The blonde let out a hoot like a goosed owl and leaned against the counter, giggling. When she got her breath back she cracked him on the arm and said, "God, Bernie, you're so *funny!*"

"Yeah," Bernie said. "Ain't that a pisser?"

"You make my sides hurt."

"Yeah," Bernie said. "So did you hear about the two old ladies walking along the beach one day? They think it's deserted, see, they're just out for a little air; but they come around this rock, there's a guy lying there on a blanket and he's naked."

"Naked," the waitress said, nodding. She had started to giggle again in anticipation.

"Yeah. One of them nudists, you know? So the two old broads stop and one of them points. The guy's lying on his back so you know what she's pointing at, right?"

"Right." More giggles. "Oh, sure."

"Well, she points and she says to the other old lady, 'You know,' she says, 'life sure is funny. When I was ten I didn't know that thing existed. When I was twenty I was curious about it. When I was thirty I was enjoying it. When I was forty I was asking for it. When I was fifty I was begging for it. When I was sixty I was paying for it. And now that I'm seventy—' "

"Right, now that she's seventy . . ."

" 'Now that I'm seventy,' she says, 'when my life is almost over, there it is growing wild.' "

The waitress thought that was the funniest one yet; she let out two hoots this time and convulsed into gales of laughter. Tears rolled down her cheeks. As far as she was concerned, old Bernie was Johnny Carson and Bob Hope and Bob Newhart all rolled up into one.

"Ain't that a *pisser?*" Bernie said.

I was leaning against the counter by this time, not ten feet away, but they still didn't seem to know I was there. I waited until the blonde got herself under control again and then rapped on the formica to get her attention. She looked at me, hiccupped, said, "Just a second, okay?" and went right on giggling.

Bernie had turned on his stool and was grinning at me. "You hear that one?" he said. "Wasn't that a pisser?"

"Yeah," I said. "If it was any more of a pisser I'd have wet my pants."

He didn't like that; his grin disappeared. Which was all right with me. I don't like stupid jokes, especially stupid Italian jokes, and I don't like the kind of people who tell them. Bernie was a jerk. And if he wanted me to, I was more than willing to tell him so.

But it didn't come to that. Whatever else Bernie was, he wasn't the belligerent type. All he did was pick up the glass of cola in front of him and mutter, "Some guys got no sense of humor."

The waitress said, "Bernie, I swear to God, you ought to go on TV. I really mean it." Then she wiped her face, let him have one more giggle, and came down to where I was. "What'll it be, mister?"

"Cup of coffee."

She turned to the hotplate on the back counter and poured the coffee. I had the newspaper photo out, and when she set the cup in front of me I laid the clipping beside it and tapped Charles Bradford's image with my forefinger. "Did this man happen to come in here on Tuesday afternoon between five and six o'clock?"

She bent close to squint at the photo. Then she frowned and said, "A tramp, right?"

"That's right."

"Well, a tramp *did* come in here on Tuesday afternoon," she said. "I think it was this one. It sure looks like him."

"What did he want?"

"A cup of coffee, same as you. I thought he was panhandling—they come in here and try to get a freebie sometimes—and I told him I had to see his money first. He had it in change, just barely. I made him pay me before I gave him the coffee."

"Did he want anything else?"

"Like what?"

"Information, maybe?"

"Well, yeah, he did ask directions. How come you're so interested in this tramp, anyway?"

"I'm trying to find him for his daughter," I said. "What did he want to know?"

"Where Firth Road was."

"Firth Road."

She nodded. "So I told him, and he drank his coffee and left. That's all."

"He didn't say what he wanted on Firth Road?"

"No. He didn't say anything else."

"What sort of street is it? A side road, a main thoroughfare, what?"

"It's only a couple of blocks long," she said. "A dead-end street."

"What's on it? Houses, businesses?"

"I don't know," she said. "Hey, Bernie, what's on Firth Road?"

Bernie turned on his stool again. He still seemed a little hurt that I hadn't properly appreciated his jokes. "Not much on it," he said in a grudging way. "PG and E substation, couple of business places, and the railroad museum."

"Railroad museum?" I asked.

"Yeah. Guy named Dallmeyer runs it. It's a freaking tourist trap."

"How long has it been there?"

"Who knows? Ten years, maybe."

"What're the business places?"

"Electrical outfit—Jorgensen's," he said. "And a fruit packing plant."

"That's all?"

"Ain't that enough?"

"How long have those two been operating?"

"How should I know? Do I look like I work for the goddamn Chamber of Commerce?"

The waitress giggled again. Even when he wasn't telling dumb jokes, Bernie was so *funny*.

I said, "How do I get to Firth Road?"

"It's a couple of miles north of here," the blonde said, "out toward the dam. It branches off the main drag."

"Oro Dam Boulevard, you mean?"

"Yeah."

"Okay. Thanks."

I drank some of my coffee; it wasn't very good, but at least it was hot. I fished two quarters out of my pocket, set them on the counter, drank a little more coffee, and got up from my stool.

"Hey, Lynn," Bernie said abruptly. "I got another one for you."

The waitress said, "Oh God," and winked at me, and went down to where he was. "Well?"

"So Smokey the Bear gets married," he said, "but he and his wife never have any sex. You know why?" But he was looking at me as he spoke, not her, and there was a determined expression on his face, as if his reputation as a comedian was on the line and he had to tell one that would make me laugh or lose points.

"No," the blonde said, "why do Smokey the Bear and his wife never have any sex?"

"Because every time she gets hot, he throws dirt on her and beats her with a shovel."

That was a one-hooter for the blonde. She said, "Nobody better try'n throw dirt on *me* when I get hot," and broke up again.

I just looked at Bernie. Then I turned and started for the door.

"You know how many Polacks it takes to pull off a kidnapping?" he said, a little desperately.

"No," the waitress said, "how many?"

"Six. One to grab the victim and five to write the ransom note."

She hooted—and I walked out into the good, clean air and shut the door quietly behind me.

10

The two-block length of Firth Road was flanked by shade trees and looked as deserted as most of the rest of Oroville. The electrical outfit, Jorgensen Electric, and the Orchard-Sweet fruit packing plant were situated across from each other in the first block; the strong, pungent smell of cooked apples and plums came out of the big warehouse there. On the second block the Pacific Gas & Electric substation and the railroad museum were also set opposite each other, with the museum on the north side. Beyond the dead-end of the street, and some dense shrubbery and scrub pine, I could see the raised right-of-way of a main line of rail tracks.

I decided to start with the substation. But if there was anyone on duty inside, I couldn't raise him. I gave it up after a time and crossed to the museum.

It was a good-sized complex set behind a wire-mesh fence: a big, high-domed roundhouse, a smaller outbuilding that looked to be some kind of storage shed, two old passenger coaches and a caboose arranged in front of and alongside the roundhouse for touring purposes, and the remains of a spur track at the rear that had probably once connected with the rail lines beyond. A sign on the front gate said the same thing as one I'd passed out on Oro Dam Boulevard: ROUNDHOUSE RAILROAD MUSEUM. Another sign below it read: RELICS OF THE FABULOUS AGE OF STEAM RAILROADING. ADMISSION $1.00. But the gate was closed and locked, and so was the ticket booth just inside, and there was a third sign on the booth that said: CLOSED.

On the east side of the complex, outside the fence and shaded by live oaks, was a small cottage that probably belonged to the man who ran the museum—Dallmeyer, Bernie the comic said his name was. Parked near it on a diagonal was a van with the museum's name painted on the side. I started back there, following a rutted gravel drive that skirted the edge of the fence. As I did I noticed that there were puffs of white vapor coming up from behind the roundhouse. At first I thought it was smoke; then I saw how quickly it evaporated and realized it was steam.

When I got to within thirty yards of the cottage I could see that the rear engine doors of the roundhouse were open; the steam was billowing out from inside. Ahead, a side gate appeared in the fence. I stopped when I got to it, because its fork latch was in place but its padlock was hooked open through the wire to one side. I hesitated, glancing at the cottage. Nobody came out of it. After ten seconds or so I shrugged, lifted the fork latch, and went through the gate and across toward the open engine doors.

As I neared them I could hear the sharp hiss of escaping steam and other sounds that meant a steam locomotive's boiler had been fired: the stuttering clamor of valves, the staccato beat of the exhaust. The locomotive, I saw a moment later, was an old Baldwin that had to have been built during the twenties; it was sitting on a turntable a dozen yards inside the roundhouse. Overhead lights blazed, giving me a clear look at the rest of the cavernous interior: whitewashed walls, swept floors, trusses, gleaming engine pits; and along the walls, tool bins and racks and workbenches, plus a number of glass-fronted cases containing historical photographs, small equipment such as reflector lanterns and switch keys, and posters, timetables, uniform caps and badges, and other memorabilia.

Through the locomotive's narrow, oblong, front glass panel, I could see a man working inside the cab. He didn't seem to see me, though; he was intent on what he was doing. I waited another ten seconds, then walked over to where I could look up through the gangway to the deck inside.

The guy up there was stoking the firebox—using a fireman's shovel to scoop coal out of the tender, then pivoting and driving one foot against a floor pedal to open the butterfly doors and feed the coal to the blaze within. He was fiftyish, thick through the shoulders and hips, with a mop of gray-flecked hair, shaggy brows, and a full beard; the rest of his face was heat-reddened and sweaty. He wore a long leather fireman's apron to protect his clothing from coal dust and cinders.

"Hello!" I called to him. "Hello in the cab!"

He heard me above the thrumming of the boiler and the throb of the valves, and whirled toward the gangway with the shovel cocked in front of his body. He stared at me for a couple of seconds. Then his surprise gave way to anger and he said, "Christ! You scared hell out of me. How did you get in here?"

"Through the side gate. It was unlocked. I'm sorry if I—"

"You're trespassing, you know that?"

"Yes, and I apologize. Are you Mr. Dallmeyer?"

"That's right. What do you want?"

"I'd like to ask you a few questions, if you don't

mind," I said. "I'm trying to find a man named Bradford, Charles Bradford. A hobo who dropped off a freight in the WP yards two days ago."

He gawped at me again out of bright gray eyes. "Why're you looking for a hobo? You a policeman?"

"No, it's nothing like that. A couple of San Francisco reporters were up here doing a feature story on modern hoboes. Bradford got his picture taken, and his daughter saw it when it appeared in the paper. I'm trying to locate him for her."

"Well, what makes you think he'd have come out here?"

"I've traced him as far as Firth Road," I said. "At least, it seems this is where he came on Tuesday afternoon."

"What time on Tuesday afternoon?"

"Sometime between five and six."

"I wasn't here then," Dallmeyer said. "I closed up at four-thirty; I had to drive down to Yuba City to pick up some Southern Pacific dining-car relics for the museum."

"What time did you get back, if you don't mind my asking?"

"It was almost midnight."

I nodded. "Would you mind taking a look at Bradford's photograph, just for the record?"

"I suppose not. But I haven't seen any tramps hanging around here, I can tell you that right now. I'd have run them off if I had. They're bad for my business."

"Sure, I understand."

He propped the shovel against the side bulkhead, wiped his hands on a rag from the engineer's seat, and then swung down off the running board. His face was still red and damp with perspiration. I gave him the *Examiner* photo, pointing out which of the men was Bradford. He looked at it, shook his head, and said, "No, I never saw him before. I never saw any of these men before."

I took the clipping back and put it into my shirt pocket.

"Can't imagine what a hobo would be doing way out here," Dallmeyer said. "They all hop the freights over by the WP yards; hardly ever this far out. How'd you trace this Bradford to Firth Road, anyhow?"

"It was a pretty complicated procedure, Mr. Dallmeyer," I said. "And I've taken up enough of your time. I'd better be on my way."

"Well, I'll walk out to the gate with you. I must have forgotten to lock it and I don't like to leave it open like that."

We left the roundhouse and went across the yard to the gate, where I apologized again for the trespass. He said, "No problem. I hope you find that hobo you're looking for." Then he let me out and padlocked the gate latch. He was already back inside the roundhouse by the time I reached the end of the gravel drive.

I walked up to the next block and entered Jorgensen Electric. The owner, Eric Jorgensen, was a fat jowly man in his late fifties who looked like a Boston bull terrier. "Nope," he said when I asked him about Bradford. "Didn't see any tramps while I was here on Tuesday. I'd have sure noticed one, too. But I left about half past four; he could have come after that."

"You closed up for the day at four-thirty, you mean?"

"Nope. Tris did that at half past five, like always."

"Who would Tris be?"

"Girl who answers the phone and waits on customers and does my books for me. Tris Wilson, my brother's girl."

Jorgensen was the only person in evidence at the moment. I asked, "Is she here now?"

"Yep. Using the can. Tris spends more time in the can than a bad burglar with a bladder problem." He thought that was funny and laughed to prove it. I let him have a small smile, which was more than I'd done for Bernie; Jorgensen, at least, was not a jerk.

It was not long before Tris, who turned out to be a plain-looking brunette in her middle twenties, came back from the can. She looked at the photo, looked at it again, gnawed on her lower lip, and said at length, "Well, I don't know. It *might* have been the same fellow. I only saw him for a moment."

"Ma'am?"

"Through the window." She nodded toward the plate-glass window that took up the left-hand wall flanking the entrance door. "I was just getting ready to close up and I happened to glance out and there he was."

"Which way was he heading?"

"West, I think."

"On this side of the street?"

"No, on the other side."

"Do you have any idea where he might have gone?"

"No," she said. "I noticed him because he looked like a hobo and you don't see many of them out here. But he wasn't doing anything out of the ordinary, just walking along, and it was closing time and I was in a hurry because I had a date. I just didn't pay that much attention to him."

"How long after you saw him did you leave the shop?"

"About five minutes, I guess."

"And he wasn't anywhere around then?"

"Well, if he was I didn't see him."

I thanked her and Jorgensen and went outside again. The Orchard-Sweet packing plant loomed across the street; I walked over there and inside the warehouse. It smelled almost overpoweringly of cooked fruit, like the pervasive odor of aging wine in a winery. None of the dozen or so employees seemed bothered by it, though. You probably wouldn't even notice it if you'd been working there for any length of time.

I showed the clipping around—it was starting to get worn from all the handling—but all I got in return were headshakes and negative words. I went out through the open rear doors to where two Latino forklift operators were loading crates into a boxcar on a rail siding. They both said they didn't know nothing about no bums, man.

And that seemed to be that. Firth Road looked like a dead-end in more ways than one.

Yet if Tris Wilson was a reliable witness, and I judged that she was, I had definitely established that Bradford *had* been out here at five-thirty on Tuesday afternoon. Why had he come here? Who was it he'd wanted to see?

I only had one lead left to pursue—those microfilm files of the *Los Angeles Times* at the library. If I couldn't find the needle in that haystack I had two choices: I could hang around Oroville and keep flashing Bradford's photo in the hope that somebody recognized him and could tell me where he'd gone; or I could call Miss A. Bradford, admit defeat, and head back home to San Francisco. I doubted if I would do the latter, though, at least not right away. Now that I was back in harness, it would be damned frustrating to have to walk away empty-handed on my first new case. Bad for business, too, if word got around.

Well, there was no point in worrying about any of that until the time came. Right now, there was the library.

11

Mrs. Kennedy took me into the microfilm room, an air-conditioned cubicle at the rear of the library, and plunked me down in front of one of those magnifying machines that look like hair dryers. Then she brought me the tapes for the August and September 1967 issues of the L.A. *Times,* showed me how to thread the machine, and left me alone.

I started with the first of August and worked ahead chronologically, skipping the want ads, the sports and fashion and business sections and concentrating on the news and feature pages, because the odds were better that Bradford had been after something there. I paid particular attention to the more unusual local items—crimes, personal tragedies, bizarre accidents, acts of heroism, political and business scandals, things like that.

At the end of an hour and a half I had reached August 31 and all I had to show for the effort was a headache; the damn screen on the viewing machine was scratched, the light was too glary, and the pages came through blurred so that you had to squint to read the newsprint. There was no mention of Charles Bradford anywhere. Nobody named McGhan, Dallmeyer, Jorgensen, or Tris Wilson—or, for that matter, Coleman, Baxter, or Mrs. Kennedy—was mentioned either. Oroville appeared a couple of times, once in the case of a hobo who'd been found stabbed in an empty boxcar, but there wasn't any connection in that that I could find. The guy who'd done the stabbing, another tramp with a felony record, had been arrested the following day.

I rolled the last of the August tapes out of the machine, then got up muttering to myself and took a couple of turns around the room to give my eyes a rest and ease the knotted muscles in my shoulders and neck. My left arm and hand were starting to cramp up again, too. I thought: This is a waste of time. Bradford could have been looking for anything, even a business advertisement or somebody's recipe for clam chowder. You'll never find it this way, groping for it blind.

Yeah, I thought then, wearily. And went back to the machine and began cranking through September 1967.

And got lucky, by God, and found it.

September 9, page eleven. In a story under a two-column headline that read: TWO DIE IN MALIBU SHOOTING. It was a love-triangle thing; a guy named Lester Raymond, who worked for one of the oil companies, had followed his wife out to the Malibu beach house of an architect named Peter Hawes, caught her and Hawes in bed together, and blown both of them away with a .45 caliber "Korean War souvenir." One of Hawes' neighbors had heard the shots, seen Raymond run out of the beach house, and got the license number of his car when he sped away. The police had not found him at the time the story was written. What caught and held my attention was a paragraph on Raymond's background near the end of the account.

> Raymond was described by friends as having a violent temper. An avid builder of model railroads, he was arrested for assaulting and threatening to kill a fellow enthusiast during a dispute at a West Covina model railroaders convention in 1962. . . .

Quickly I cranked the film ahead to September 10. The follow-up story said that Raymond had still not been apprehended. It also said that he had apparently managed to make off with thirty thousand dollars in cash and another seventy thousand in negotiable securities belonging to Peter Hawes. There was some mystery as to why Hawes had had that much money lying around his house, which probably meant that there was something illegal or at least shady about it.

September 11. Raymond was still at large. The police lieutenant in charge of the investigation had "no comment to make at this time" on the missing money and securities. There was another mention of Raymond's hobby: he had belonged to a Los Angeles-based model railroad club called the Cannonballers.

The September 12 edition had nothing about the case. I kept cranking. What I was looking for now was a photograph of Lester Raymond; the *Times* doesn't use that many photos with its crime coverage, and there hadn't been one accompanying any of the previous three accounts. There wasn't any with the story I found in the September 13 edition either, but the emphasis there had shifted from Raymond to the reasons for Peter Hawes having $100,000 on hand. According to the police, Hawes had intended to use the money to make a narcotics buy—heroin and marijuana; they had linked him to a group that was smuggling the stuff in from Mexico. Hawes was described as "an alleged supplier of drugs to professional and film people in the Malibu area." Raymond, as far as anybody knew, was still a fugitive.

There were two more stories, one on September 14 following up on the drug angle and the last, little more than a squib, on September 16; the only new information they contained was the fact that Raymond's car had been found abandoned on a sidestreet in Ventura. And that was it. Raymond and the missing money were not mentioned again in September, which meant that he hadn't been apprehended during the rest of that month. When *had* the authorities caught up with him? I wondered.

Or had they caught up with him at all?

I rewound the spool of microfilm, shut off the machine. And sat there brooding. And after a time something jogged in my memory, something the WP yardmaster, Coleman, had said to me when I asked if he'd been at the yard around three on Tuesday afternoon: *I was. Out by the freight storage shed, as I recall, discussing a shipment of wheel flanges with a local businessman.* Wheel flanges—yeah. I began to get it then. I didn't like it much, but I could see the way the whole thing with Charles Bradford on Tuesday *might* have happened.

But I needed more information before I could be sure enough to do anything about it. I went out front and got Mrs. Kennedy's permission to make a collect call on the telephone in her office. It was after seven o'clock now; Arleen Bradford would be long gone from Denim, Inc. I dialed her home number, went through the usual rigmarole with the long-distance operator. And the line was busy.

I hunted up Mrs. Kennedy again and asked for the files of Oroville's city directory. What I was looking for appeared in the directory for 1972. All right. I returned to her office and tried Arleen Bradford's number again. This time, the line was clear; Miss Bradford answered on the third ring and agreed to accept the charges.

"Have you found my father yet?" she asked immediately. There was more eagerness in her voice than she might have been willing to admit to.

"Not yet, no. But he may still be here in Oroville and I'm on his trail."

"Then why did you call?"

"To ask you some questions that might be important. You told me yesterday that your father belonged to a model railroad club in Los Angeles. What was the name of the club? Was it the Cannonballers?"

"I don't understand," she said. "What does that have to do with—"

"Please, Miss Bradford. Just answer my question. *Was* your father's club the Cannonballers?"

"Why . . . yes, I believe it was."

"Then he must have known a man named Lester Raymond."

"Who?"

"Lester Raymond. Also a member of the Cannonballers in the late sixties. He murdered his wife and her lover in Malibu in 1967 and ran off with a hundred thousand dollars in cash and negotiable securities."

She was silent for a few seconds. Then she made a vague bewildered sound and said, "Yes. Lester Raymond . . . yes. Daddy knew him; he came to our place several times before all of that happened. But I don't—"

"You met Raymond yourself, then?"

"Of course. I was living at home at the time."

"What did he look like?"

"Big, hairy, going bald on top—one of those macho-male types." Her voice dripped disapproval.

"Was he bearded or clean-shaven?"

"Clean-shaven."

Clean-shaven and going bald, I thought. But a man could always grow a beard; and the hairpieces they had nowadays were so good you had to be an expert to tell that they weren't the real thing. I asked, "Did he have a round face, gray eyes, bushy eyebrows?"

"Yes, that sounds like him."

"Can you remember if he was ever captured?"

"I . . . don't think he was, no. Except for Hannah running off the minute she turned eighteen, he was all Daddy talked about for weeks afterward—how he'd managed to vanish into thin air. . . . Now will you please tell me what something that happened fifteen years ago has to do with my father's present whereabouts?"

"I'm not sure yet, Miss Bradford." I had no time to explain it to her and I didn't want to alarm her prematurely. "I'll call you again as soon as I have something definite to report," I said, and hung up before she could say anything else.

Dallmeyer, I thought. It's got to be Dallmeyer.

It figured this way: Lester Raymond not only manages to elude the police in 1967, he manages to alter his identity and cover his tracks so well that they're never able to trace him. That sort of thing isn't easy to do, but people have done it before—and with enough intelligence, plenty of luck, and $100,000 to make the task a little easier, Raymond gets away with it. Maybe he stays in California somewhere; more likely, he heads out of state and establishes himself in a place a few hundred or a few thousand miles away. Most men with that kind of money burning a hole in their pocket would go through it in a short period of time, but suppose Raymond has enough sense to invest it or to start a business, make the money work for him, double or triple it in a few years. He's not a professional criminal, after all; he committed murder and theft on irrational impulse, not through premeditation. Basically he's just an average citizen.

Five years pass. He figures he's home free by this time, so for whatever reason he decides to come back to California, to a small town more than six hundred miles from Los Angeles. And because he's always been interested in trains, he uses some of his capital to buy a railroad museum under the name of Dallmeyer and again settles down to the quiet life of a model citizen.

For ten years he resides in Oroville with nobody the wiser as to who he really is. But then circumstance, or fate—call it what you wanted—brings Charles Bradford here. And puts Raymond at the Western Pacific freight yards at the same time Bradford goes there from the hobo jungle to report the streamliner's theft. Wheel flanges were a railroad item; the only local businessman who was likely to order a shipment of them was the owner of a railroad museum. The logistics of it had to have worked that way.

Bradford sees Raymond talking to the yardmaster, probably without Raymond seeing him, and recognizes him. It's been fifteen years since he's laid eyes on his old friend, and Raymond has added the beard and hairpiece; but you don't forget what your friends look like, particularly one as notorious as Lester Raymond. Still, Bradford isn't completely sure, so he doesn't approach Raymond in the yards. Maybe he hangs around long enough to watch Raymond drive away in that van with the name of the museum on it; that's how he knows where to go looking for him later on. Then Bradford heads for the library to check past city directories to find out how long the Roundhouse Museum has been in operation, and to refresh his memory on the details of Raymond's fifteen-year-old crime in Malibu.

When he leaves the library Bradford heads out to Firth Road to confront his former pal. Object: blackmail. Not major blackmail, necessarily; maybe Bradford is only after a few bucks and a hot meal. But he's after *something*. He's down-and-out and maybe bitter about it, and he's gone to too much trouble to be looking up a fugitive murderer because of simple curiosity or for old time's sake.

What was it Kerry had said to me last night, the line from the poem about hoboes? *Each man's grave is his own affair*. Yeah. Hannah Peterson had told me her father didn't care about money, was only interested in the adventurous hobo life. A fat lot greedy Hannah Peterson knew. In more ways than one, she was her father's daughter.

But the real irony was that Bradford hadn't known there was twenty thousand dollars waiting for him from his late uncle's estate; that he didn't *have* to resort to blackmail to get money, to maybe turn his life around. . . .

Without more facts, that was as far as I could piece things together. What had happened after Bradford arrived at Firth Road was still a mystery. But it figured to be one of two things. The first was that Raymond had paid him off and Bradford had left Oroville for parts unknown—that he'd received enough money to take a bus instead of a freight train, or maybe even to have bought a secondhand car. The other possibility was a hell of a lot grimmer.

The other possibility was murder.

Raymond had a violent temper; he had killed twice

before when that temper was aroused. It was plenty possible that Bradford's blackmail demand, particularly if it was for a substantial amount of cash, had bought him a bullet or a cracked head instead. I hoped that wasn't the way it had been, but I had an uneasy hunch that it was.

There wasn't any basis for the hunch . . . or maybe there was. Something had begun to scratch at the back of my mind, something about my own meeting with Raymond/Dallmeyer that hadn't been quite right. . . .

And then I knew what it was, and the skin along my back tightened and began to crawl. "Jesus," I said aloud. "Sweet Jesus!"

I jumped up from the desk and ran out through the main part of the library, startling Mrs. Kennedy and a couple of patrons. I should have gone straight to the local police with it—but telling them the whole story, convincing them to question the man they knew as Dallmeyer and search the museum, would take too much time. Hours, maybe. By then it would be too late. It might already be too late, but there was still a chance that it wasn't. I *had* to go out to Firth Road myself.

12

It was dusk when I made the turn off Oro Dam Boulevard, shut off my headlights, and drove slowly toward the museum complex. Nightlights burned on poles inside the wire-mesh fence; there were lights on inside the roundhouse, too, and in one of the facing windows of the cottage at the rear. The van I had seen earlier was still parked on the same diagonal back there.

I drove past the entrance, peering over at the museum yard. There was no sign of Raymond. Near the dead-end barrier, an unpaved drive angled alongside the PG&E sub-station; I pulled up there and left the car in the shadows behind the building, where it couldn't be seen from across the street. Then I moved over into the trees and under-brush that flanked the railroad right-of-way, and cautiously worked my way parallel to the museum fence until I got to where I could see the back of the roundhouse.

The engine doors were still open. The interior lights let me see the Baldwin locomotive's cowcatcher and part of her blunt nose. There was no longer any steam coming out of the exhaust, and the boiler had been shut down; no sounds drifted over from there, or from anywhere else in the vicinity. If Raymond was inside the roundhouse he was doing something pretty quiet.

He was inside, all right; I had been standing there waiting and watching for five minutes when he appeared alongside the locomotive and came walking outside. He paused long enough to light a cigar, take a couple of deep puffs on it. Then he went across the yard to the side gate, unlocked it, stepped through, locked it again behind him, and vanished into the shadows fronting the cottage.

He would be coming back to the roundhouse sooner or later, though; otherwise he wouldn't have left the engine doors open or the lights on. I would have to hurry. And I would have to be damned careful while I was poking around inside there. I didn't have a gun and it seemed likely that he did. I did not want to end up where I was afraid Charles Bradford had.

Quickly, I went back along the fence to a point where the high bulk of the roundhouse loomed between me and the cottage. A long time ago, a tree had fallen against the fence here; the wire mesh was bent inward slightly and flattened down and rusted at the top. Somebody had come out with a power saw and cut the tree into six-foot segments, also a long time ago, because the segments were still scattered over the ground and starting to rot. One of them lay close to the fence; when I got up on the decaying log I could reach the tubular top bar and get enough of a grip on it to haul myself up.

The problem was, I couldn't maintain much of a hold with the crabbed fingers on my left hand and I had to do most of the work with my right, clenching my teeth against the pain. It took me a good three minutes of grunting and heaving to hoist my fat backside over the bar and drop down on the other side. The noise I made doing it seemed loud enough to alert half the town, but that was a product of tension and my heightened senses. The cottage was two hundred yards away, and the sounds wouldn't have carried that far.

Still, I ran ahead to where one of the old passenger coaches was set roughly parallel to the back wall of the roundhouse. I knelt along the coach's front end, massaging my cramped hand, flexing it. I listened and watched the cottage for more than a minute before I was satisfied Raymond wasn't coming back to investigate.

All right. I moved back to the other end of the car, crossed to the roundhouse's side wall, then went forward again to the rear corner. Still no movement over at the cottage. I slipped around the corner, ducked inside through the open door.

And stopped in front of the turntable and tried to keep from gagging. There was a burnt-meat smell in the air, faint but nauseatingly pungent. That told me all I needed to know; I was too late, all right, but not by much more than an hour.

I went ahead anyway, around on the right side of the Baldwin and then up through the gangway and inside the cab. The smell, as I had known it would be, was coming from inside the firebox. I did not want to pedal open the butterfly doors and look inside, but I steeled myself, breathing through my mouth, and did it just the same.

There wasn't anything left to see—just the glowing embers of the coal fire spread out over the grate. The body of Charles Bradford had long since been reduced to ashes.

If you kept stoking the fire in one of these steam boilers, you could get it as hot as an old-fashioned crematorium.

That was what Raymond had been doing when I interrupted him earlier. And that was what had happened to me back at the library, the thing in retrospect that hadn't been quite right. It had been late afternoon, Raymond had closed the museum for the day, but there he was, feeding coal into the box as if he'd been preparing to take this old hog for a run. But there wasn't anywhere to take it; and you don't stoke the boiler full up on a relic like this just to check the steam pressure or how the valves are working. Christ knew where he'd had the body stashed then—not up in the cab, or he'd have been more nervous than he was, but probably somewhere close by.

I took my foot off the floor pedal, and the doors snapped shut, and I started to turn away. Something that gleamed dully on the deck caught my eye; it was under the fireman's seat, up against the footboard. I squatted on my heels and scraped it out and held it up in my palm.

It was a piece of copper, elliptical in shape, about three inches long, with some sort of design etched into the metal; through an eye at the top was a broken length of thin chain.

Bradford's pendant, the one Arleen had made for him back in high school.

That put the clincher on things. The chain must have caught on something and broken when Raymond stuffed Bradford's body inside the firebox; he hadn't noticed the pendant there on the deck afterward. I straightened, still trying not to gag, and put it into my pocket. The charred-flesh smell was making me nauseous. Raymond must be a cold-blooded bastard to have hung around in here after the cremation.

Well, he wasn't going to get away with murder this time. I had plenty enough evidence now to bring the local cops out here and have him arrested. And plenty enough to convict him of a third count of willful homicide.

I turned into the gangway. Outside, a long way off, a locomotive's air horn cut into the early-evening stillness—probably a freight coming into Oroville from the north. I dropped off the running board and swung toward the open doors.

And Raymond was there, just walking into view on the gravel outside.

He saw me at the same time and came to a sudden halt. There was a frozen moment during which we both stared at each other. He didn't have a weapon of any kind, at least not in either of his hands. The air horn wailed again, and I thought: Goddamn it! and Raymond made a noise like an animal and turned and ran.

I pounded after him, cursing myself for not having got out of here sooner. The side gate stood open now and he was heading straight for it. Heading for the cottage, I thought, going after a gun. I wasn't in very good physical shape, but neither was he—a couple of overweight middle-aged guys unused to this kind of exertion. He stumbled just after he got through the gate, and I caught him ten steps beyond.

I hit him from behind with my right shoulder and forearm, sent him sprawling. But the impact and my own momentum threw me off stride, too, and I went down on top of him just as he started to roll away. We flipped over together, clawing at each other, grunting like two pigs in a wallow. Pain erupted the length of my bad arm; gravel gouged into my body and the side of my face, stinging.

When we came up we were both on our knees. He broke loose of me and swung at my head, and even though I saw it coming and tried to duck away, the blow caught me over the left ear and knocked me flat again.

He scrambled to his feet, staggering, turning. But I was already heaving up onto all fours, with my head full of buzzing noises and my left arm half numb, and I was between him and the cottage. He might have charged me, tried to take me in a hand-to-hand fight, but he didn't do it. He had no way of knowing about my bad arm, and maybe he sensed that I might be the stronger; or maybe panic had hold of him and he was not thinking at all. Whatever the reason, he turned his back to me and ran again—away from the cottage, back along the fence toward the woods at the rear of the museum grounds.

I tried to get up too fast, lost my footing and toppled forward like an old tree, scraping skin off my right palm. By the time I made it to my feet again, he was thirty yards away and crashing through the underbrush that grew in close to the fence. I lumbered after him, panting and wheezing, with a chest pain starting that put a peripheral fear of a heart attack into my head.

Tree shadows swallowed him, but I could still hear him thrashing around in the underbrush. Just before I reached the woods I became aware of a rumbling, rattling noise and the ground seemed to vibrate a little. Then the air horn bellowed again, and through the trees I could see the Cyclopean glare of a locomotive's headlight as the southbound freight clattered into view on the right-of-way. The sweep of light also let me see Raymond: he was running straight toward the tracks and the oncoming freight.

The train was not going very fast, throttled way down and crawling along the tangent, and when he scrambled up the incline I knew what he was going to do. The locomotive and its light swept on past; a short string of flats followed it. I came out of the trees just as the first of a line of boxcars drew abreast of him. He tried to catch hold of the iron ladder on the side of one, missed it, almost fell, and then straightened in time to lunge at the next in line. He caught hold of the ladder on that one, but by that time I was a couple of strides behind him, running sideways on the packed earth of the incline.

It was a foolish thing to do, but I grabbed onto the ladder, too, with my good right hand. Even as slow as the freight was traveling, its momentum almost jerked my arm out of its socket, almost tore my fingers loose from the rung; if that had happened I might have fallen under the wheels. But I managed to hang on, to get one foot anchored on the bottom rung an instant after Raymond hoisted himself up and through the open door of the car. And I swung in right on his heels, barreled into him as soon as he let go of the ladder and his feet hit the swaying floorboards.

The boxcar was empty; the odor of dust and apples assaulted my nostrils as we smacked together, tumbled to the floor. The collision broke us apart, and for two or three seconds I couldn't find him in the darkness. Then I heard him scrabbling around on my left, and lunged in that direction, and my good hand scraped across his shirtfront. The material ripped, but I got hold of him anyway and hauled him in against me. We rolled over a couple of times, his breath exploding sourly into my face, his fingers clawing at my cheek. I came up on top and swung down at him, a blind, wild swing, then flailed at him again.

That second blow took him somewhere on the head; he grunted in pain. I hit him a second time, more solidly than the first. He stiffened under me and I knew he was hurt and I thought I had him. But one of his hands clutched at my groin, found enough purchase to make me cry out and try to twist aside. I pawed at his hand to keep him from rupturing me, and he swatted me in the ribs with his other arm, and the next thing I knew I was over on my back and he was pinning me with the bulk of his upper body, fumbling at my neck with both hands. I kicked at him, didn't connect; missed with an awkward punch. And by then it was too late: he had his fingers wrapped around my neck in a stranglehold.

He slammed my head against the floorboards, did it again, did it a third time . . .

Pain. Disorientation. A sudden feeling of distance and time-stoppage, as if part of my mind had been jarred out of whack. I couldn't move; I couldn't seem to breathe either. A thought came out of the swirling black inside my head: *He paralyzed me!* I screamed in rage and terror, but the scream was inside my head too, and it had no voice.

Raymond let go of my neck; I felt his weight lift off me, heard him panting, dimly saw him get to his feet and brace himself against the sway of the car. He was giant then, looming, swaying—a massive silhouette outlined against blobs and flickers of light, against a blur of confused shapes sliding past the open door. He kept staring down at me, and I thought through sweeps of pain: Move! He'll kill you if you don't move. But except for helpless little twitches, I could not make my body respond.

He turned away abruptly, lurched over to the door and leaned out. The blobs and flickers of light, the blur of shapes, were slowing down. He glanced back at me again, hesitated—and disappeared. Now you see him, now you don't. Gone. Poof, like magic stuff.

Jumped off, I thought. For God's sake, *move!*

But all I could do was lie there, jouncing and swaying and twitching. Slowing down like the train. Going away like Raymond. Going, going . . .

Gone.

13

There was light shining in my eyes. I reached up and swiped at it, the way you'd try to brush away an insect. But the light would not go away; it just kept shining, hot and bright, burning into my skull like some kind of powerful laser beam.

Somebody said, "Come on, 'bo, wake up. You can't sleep here. This ain't a frigging hotel."

I turned my head to one side, to avoid the light, and realized I was lying still: no more jouncing and swaying. I opened my eyes. Dusty floorboards came into focus in a wide splash of light. Boxcar. Raymond. Christ, Raymond!

I rolled over and tried to lift up; my left arm was numb and wouldn't support me and I sprawled face down. When I tried it again I used my right hand, and this time I made it up onto my knees. The back of my head throbbed as if somebody was beating on it with a stick. A wave of nausea washed through me; bile pumped into the back of my throat, clogged for an instant, then rose again. I knelt there with my head hanging down, vomiting.

"Drunk," a different voice said disgustedly. "You'd think these tramps would learn—"

"Wait, Frank," the first voice said. "He's not drunk—he's hurt. Look at the back of his head."

Part of the light moved at the same time I finished emptying my stomach. "You're right. Shit, it looks stove in."

"No, it's not that bad."

"Bloody as hell. Hey, 'bo, what happened? You been in a fight?"

I pawed at my mouth, got one foot down under me, and managed to heave myself upright. The boxcar's side wall, the one with the door in it, was only a couple of steps away, and that was a good thing; I would not have stayed on my feet if it had been any farther away. As it was, I hit the wall sideways and slid along it to the edge of the door, knees buckling, before I caught myself and hung on.

One of the voices said, "Hey, take it easy," and a hand grabbed hold of my shoulder to steady me. But it was the left shoulder, the bad one, and I made a noise in my throat and shook the hand off. I could see the two men now, even though both of them were still shining big electric torches at me. A different kind of light, artificial-looking and faintly greenish, spilled into the car from outside.

I looked away from them and out through the door. The freight yards. The artificial-looking light was coming from the strings of sodium vapor arcs that crisscrossed the work areas. It made the rails gleam, and for a couple of seconds I imagined they were moving, writhing along the ground like big silver snakes. The smells of oil and hot metal came to me from somewhere; I thought I was going to vomit again.

"We better get him some first-aid, Frank," one of the men said. Yard bulls, that was what they were. Railroad security cops. "He needs a doctor."

"Yeah."

No, I thought, get the police, I got to talk to the police. I tried to say the words, but they seemed to lodge in my throat like fragments of bone. Something wrong with my voice. Something wrong with my head, too. It ached like fury; the pain was so sharp I couldn't think straight.

Shit, it looks stove in . . .

I put my hand back there: wet, pulpy. Jesus! I pulled the hand down and looked at it, and the fingers were stained with smears of blood; the artificial light made the stains look dark and unreal, like shadows clinging to my fingers.

My knees buckled again. One of the bulls caught hold of me, braced my body against his. "Easy, 'bo," he said.

"We'll get you mixed up. You'll be okay."

"Can he walk?" the other one asked.

"If he can't we'll have to carry him to the first-aid station."

I got a word out; it sounded thick and clotted like the blood on my head. "No . . ."

"Don't try to talk. Frank, jump down and take his legs."

"Police," I said, "call the police."

"Sure. After we get you a doctor."

"No, the police. Quick. He'll get away . . ."

"Who'll get away?"

"Raymond. No, Dallmeyer."

"Somebody must have robbed him," the other one, Frank, said from outside. He was down on the ground now, looking up at me. "Goddamn jackrollers."

"Listen," I said, "you got to listen. Not robbery—murder. He killed Bradford."

"Murder?" the bull holding me said.

"The police, call the police."

"All right, we'll call them. You let us take care of you first. Okay?"

"Yeah," I said. "Okay."

The hands shifted, slid around under my armpits. He lifted me, and Frank took hold of my legs, and they lowered me down out of the car. I could stand up all right, but Frank yelled, "Hey, you guys give me some help," and pretty soon two other men were there and more hands were supporting me. The first bull jumped down. He had a handlebar mustache, the biggest one I'd ever seen; I found myself gawping at it.

"You boys take him to first-aid," he said. "I'll notify Buckner."

The hands moved me away, half-carrying me. I had a confused impression of lights, rail cars, gleaming tracks, corrugated-iron buildings; of faces and orange hard hats and muttered voices. Then we were inside one of the buildings, and there was a cot, and they made me lie down on my stomach. Somebody said, "Holy Mother, will you look at that?" and somebody else said, "Get some antiseptic—quick."

Sharp stinging pain.

I yelled—and blacked out again.

When I came out of it there was another light shining in my eyes—a pen-flash this time. I was still lying on the cot, turned on my side now with my right cheek against a pillow. The guy with the light was standing over me. "No, don't close your eyes," he said. "Keep looking at the light."

"Doctor?"

"Yes. Do you feel nauseous?"

"A little."

"Need to vomit?"

"No."

"Can you see me clearly? Any double vision?"

"No. I can see you."

"Do you know where you are?"

"Freight yards," I said. My head still ached hellishly, but most of the disorientation seemed to be gone. I told him that. I told him my name, too, for good measure.

"Can you remember what happened to you?"

"Yeah," I said, "I remember."

He stepped back. "Let's see if you can sit up."

It took me a few seconds, but I managed it. The room swam a little at first, then settled into focus and stayed that way. There were three other men in it: the yard bull with the handlebar mustache, a thick-necked guy wearing one of the orange hard hats, and a heavyset, graying policeman in uniform.

The doctor put the light in my eyes again for a couple of seconds, switched it off. He was middle-aged and trim, the kind who probably played tennis as well as golf. "Mild nausea," he said, to the others as well as to me. "Slight dilation of the right pupil. No apparent retrograde amnesia. Concussion, certainly, but it doesn't appear to be any more serious than that."

I said, "All the blood . . ."

"Skin lacerations. You have a bad bruise, too. I'll have an X ray taken at the hospital to be sure the skull isn't damaged."

"Hospital?"

"Yes. For the X ray and to have your wounds treated properly."

"What time is it?"

He frowned. The thick-necked guy took out a railroad pocket watch, looked at it, and said, "Quarter past ten."

More than two hours since I'd had my run-in with Lester Raymond. Damn! "I can't go to the hospital right now," I said. I gestured toward the uniformed cop. "I need to talk to the police. It's urgent."

The four of them held a short conference. Then the doctor went away, still frowning; the yard bull went with him. But the thick-necked guy stayed.

The cop said, "I'm Sergeant Collins, Oroville police. This is Mr. Buckner, the night yardmaster here."

"I'm a private investigator," I said. "But I guess you know that by now."

He nodded. "We looked at your ID. You're the man who was in to see Sergeant Huddleston this afternoon, the one who turned up the kid thief."

"Right. And that's not all I turned up today."

I told him the full story of Charles Bradford and Lester Raymond, everything I knew for certain and everything I had surmised. I left nothing out, including my ill-advised excursion to the museum tonight and the rationale for it and what had happened afterward. I also gave him Bradford's pendant, which was still in my pocket.

He was not happy with any of it, but he didn't openly condemn me for my actions. Like Huddleston, he was a professional; upholding the law was more important to him than anything else.

Buckner, however, looked shocked. "By Christ," he said, "I can't believe it. I've known Jim Dallmeyer for years. Hell, we played softball together . . ."

"I know him, too," Collins said. "But maybe neither of us knows him or anybody else as well as we think we do."

"I still can't believe it."

"Well, we'll damn well check it out." Collins looked at me. "You feel up to taking a ride?"

"Down to the police station?"

"The hospital first, then the station."

"Whatever you say. But you'd better hurry. Raymond—Dallmeyer—has had better than two hours to go on the run again. He might have figured he finished me off in that boxcar, but with a triple homicide rap hanging over him, he can't take the chance. He'll be gone by the time you can get your men out to the museum."

"We'll see about that," Collins said. "If he isn't gone, if all of this is a load of crap . . ."

"Believe me, it's not a load of crap."

"For your sake, mister," he said, "it better not be."

A brace of uniformed patrolmen drove me to the hospital. Collins went elsewhere, presumably to the railroad museum to check out my story. The trim doctor was waiting for us when we arrived; he saw to it that I got my head x-rayed and partially shaved and bandaged. He seemed to prefer that I spend the night at the hospital, as a simple precaution, but he didn't put up much of an argument when the patrolmen told him their orders were to take me to the police station. I did not put up any argument at all. I had had enough of hospitals to last me the rest of my life;

just the few minutes I'd spent in this one made me twitchy, and I couldn't wait to get out of it again.

When we came into the police station, the cop manning the desk—one I had never seen before—asked me if I wanted to make a telephone call. Meaning did I want to get in touch with my lawyer. I said no. I had no reason to want to do that—not yet, anyway. So they stuffed me into one of the holding cells and left me to do my waiting alone.

The doctor had given me some pain pills at the hospital; I had already taken two, but I swallowed another one dry and then lay down on the cot. Some of the ache in my head abated after awhile, but the drugs made me drowsy. I was hanging onto the edge of sleep when the desk cop showed up again and roused me and let me out.

I got taken then to a door marked CHIEF OF POLICE. On the other side of it was a small, functional office containing nondescript furniture and two men, both of them standing: Collins, and an angular guy of about fifty with a long, narrow face and spatulate hands. The angular one's name was Lydecker, it developed. He was Oroville's chief of police.

Lydecker told me to sit down. He and Collins remained standing. "Looks like you were right about Jim Dallmeyer," he said. But he didn't sound too pleased about it.

"No sign of him at the museum?"

"No sign of him anywhere," Collins said. "His van was gone when we got there. Front door of the cottage was standing wide open. Dresser drawers pulled out, closet in the bedroom half-empty—looks like he packed and beat it in a hurry."

"Then you believe me now?"

"We believe you. We searched the place and found a couple of incriminating things—a wallet belonging to Charles Bradford, for one. We've got an APB out on Dallmeyer right now."

"But we'd have him in custody already," Lydecker said to me, "if you'd played it by the book. Christ, man, why didn't you come to us right away instead of trying to take him by yourself?"

"What can I say? I screwed up; I admit it. But I didn't go out there with the idea of tackling him myself, trying to play hero. I thought it would take too long to convince you to investigate, and I figured maybe he hadn't cremated Bradford's body yet. Proof was all I was after. I found it, too—that pendant . . ."

Lydecker was shaking his head. "You screwed up, all right," he said, "and I don't like it. On the other hand, you did turn up a homicide in my town, and a multiple killer to boot. . . . Hell, I don't know what to do about you."

I didn't say anything. Things were a little dicey now; if he wanted to make trouble for me, I stood to lose my license all over again. In fact, with the publicity this was bound to get, maybe I stood to lose it no matter what Lydecker decided to do. I could just see the headlines: PRIVATE EYE IN HOT WATER AGAIN. FIRST DAY BACK IN BUSINESS—ANOTHER HOMICIDE.

My head had begun to throb as intensely as before. My thoughts were running a little fuzzy at the edges, too. I hoped they weren't going to keep me here very long. If this session lasted much more than another fifteen minutes I was liable to fall asleep in the chair. Or fall out of the damned chair altogether.

It didn't last much longer, thank God. They had some questions for me, mainly about the details of my activities in Oroville, for clarification purposes. I did some babbling in answer to the last one Lydecker asked—I was pretty woozy by then and my mouth flapped like a ventriloquist's dummy's—and that convinced them to call a halt to the proceedings.

Evidently they had decided beforehand to put me up for the night at a local motel, rather than stick me back in the holding cell. Collins said something about the motel and took me outside to his car and drove me a short distance to a place that had a blue neon sign and some buildings arranged in a half-circle. Then we were in a room, and he said somebody would be back for me in the morning. Then I was alone, sitting on the edge of the bed. Then there was nothing—an absolute void, dreamless, that wasn't like sleep at all.

14

The young, flat-faced sergeant, Huddleston, was the one who came for me in the morning. He woke me by banging on the door, and I staggered out of bed and let him in. I must have looked pretty bad; the first thing he said was, "Man, you had it rough last night, didn't you?"

I mumbled something only half coherent, because I was still trying to fight off the loginess of sleep, and shambled into the bathroom and splashed my face with cold water. It made my teeth chatter, and that in turn made my head hurt. But it was a muted kind of aching, not unlike that of a hangover. The inside of my mouth tasted like I had swallowed something that had crawled out from under a woodpile, something nobody should ever try to eat.

Huddleston was standing in the bathroom doorway. "How do you feel?" he asked.

"I may live," I said. "I'm not sure yet."

"I had a concussion once. I know what it's like."

"Yeah."

"Yours isn't too bad, though. Hospital called to say the X ray they took turned out negative—no serious damage."

"Good. Did anybody find Raymond yet?"

"Not yet."

"Damn."

"Don't worry, he won't get away this time."

"I hope not. Okay if I take a shower?"

"Go ahead."

All I had on was my underwear; somehow I had managed to take off the rest of my clothes last night. I stripped down, turned on the shower, and got under it for about five minutes—hot, cold, hot, cold. That woke me up. I would have liked to brush my teeth, to get rid of that foul taste in my mouth; I settled instead for rinsing them with cold water from the sink tap. I caught a glimpse of myself in the medicine cabinet mirror when I was done. What I looked like was one of those sub-human types who dunked women in vats of boiling oil in the sex-and-sadism pulp magazines of the thirties.

"You're too goddamn old to take this kind of abuse," I said to my reflection. "You were better off forcibly retired, you know that? You never did know what was good for you."

When I went out into the other room Huddleston was sitting in the only chair, smoking a cigarette. He watched me pick up my shirt, find the little vial of pain capsules the doctor had given me last night, and eat two of them. Then he said, "There's an FBI agent from Sacramento waiting down at the station. He wants to talk to you."

"FBI, huh?"

"It's their baby, too, on account of Raymond leaving California with the stolen money and securities fifteen years ago. Dallmeyer is Lester Raymond, all right; his fingerprints were all over his cottage and they matched up in the FBI computer."

I had my shirt on and I was getting into my pants. "How did they know he left the state?"

"He cashed some of those negotiable securities in Las Vegas and a couple of other places back in '67 and '68," Huddleston said. "But he was slick about it—he left the FBI with a cold trail each time. Turns out he lived in Omaha and Denver before he came to Oroville ten years ago."

"Oh?"

"Sergeant Collins found evidence at the cottage that proves it. Chief Lydecker notified the Bureau last night."

"What's the word on Charles Bradford?"

"Not much doubt that Raymond killed him and cremated the body, just like you said. County lab people came down from Chico and ran tests on the ashes in the locomotive's firebox; they found bone and dental fragments."

I thought of Arleen Bradford and Hannah Peterson. "Did anybody notify Bradford's next of kin?"

"I'm not sure," he said. "Chief probably did, though. One of the reporters for the local paper got hold of the story this morning; there'll be a bunch more from the wire services and Christ knows where else in town before long. Our department wouldn't look too good if Bradford's daughters got the news from tonight's papers instead of from us."

Reporters, I thought. Ah Christ, here we go again.

"Did you want to do it?" Huddleston asked. "Tell the daughter who hired you?"

"Hell, no."

"I don't blame you. It's a lousy job. I had to tell a woman once that her two teenage kids were killed in an accident. I went out and got drunk afterward; it didn't help much."

"It never does," I said. "What about the rest of it? Am I being blamed for letting Raymond get away? Officially, I mean."

Huddleston shrugged, jabbed out his cigarette in a glass ashtray on the table beside him. "You made a mistake," he said. "So what else is new? People make mistakes every day. Important thing is, you exposed a murder—and a murderer."

"Do Lydecker and the FBI feel the same way?"

"I wouldn't worry too much about it if I were you."

I nodded, feeling better now, and finished dressing, and we left the motel. On the way downtown Huddleston asked, "You hungry?"

"Yeah. I haven't eaten in close to twenty-four hours. But mostly what I could use is some coffee."

"Plenty of coffee at the station," he said. "There's a drive-through McDonald's up ahead; I don't mind swinging by there to get you some food if you want."

"Thanks."

At the fast-food place I bought a couple of Egg McMuffins to go. When we got to the green cinder-block building that housed the police station I saw that my car was parked in one of the slots facing the river; Huddleston told me Lydecker had had it picked up and brought in last night. We went inside. The reporters hadn't shown up yet, which was a relief. The only person hanging around in there was a uniformed cop manning the duty desk.

Huddleston got me some coffee and then took me to Lydecker's office. Lydecker wasn't in it; neither was the guy from the FBI. So I got to sit there alone for ten minutes, eating my breakfast, before the grind started. That was a relief, too. I always did cope with things better on a full stomach.

The door opened finally and a tall, lean guy came inside like he owned the place. That made him FBI; they always take over like that, as if working for the government automatically gives them some sort of special gift of importance. This one's name was Dillard and he was like every FBI agent I'd ever met: of indeterminate age, clean-cut, low-key, polite, and persistent as hell. Efrem Zimbalist,

Jr., in the flesh. Living proof that once in a while Hollywood manages to get its stereotypes exactly right.

Dillard asked me two or three hundred questions, some of them twice; I answered each one in the same low-key, polite way he asked them. We got along all right as a result. I even managed to get him to tell me what it was Sergeant Collins had found at Raymond's cottage last night. Evidently Raymond had been something of a pack rat when it came to his personal papers; there had been a box full of old bills and receipts dating all the way back to 1967. The papers proved that he'd first taken up residence in Omaha, where he'd bought a garage and rented a house and lived for thirteen months. Then, for undetermined reasons, he'd sold the garage and moved to Denver and opened a hobby shop, one that had specialized in model railroading items. He'd sold that place, again for undetermined reasons, late in 1971, after which he'd come back to California and put together the railroad museum here.

As for Raymond's present whereabouts, they were still unknown. His van had been found abandoned about an hour ago in Red Bluff, some fifty miles northwest of Oroville; from there he could have hitched a ride, or hopped a bus or a freight, or stolen a car, and headed just about anywhere. The FBI and the state police were busy checking every possibility.

Dillard asked, "You have no idea where Mr. Raymond might have gone, is that correct?" Mr. Raymond. The Bureau's representatives were polite to and about everybody these days, including people who committed multiple acts of homicide.

The question was one of those he'd asked me before, and I gave him the same answer: "No. Yesterday was the first time I laid eyes on the man—the first I even knew he existed."

"He said nothing at all to you during your, ah, skirmish last night?"

"Not that I can remember."

"And the last you saw of him was when he jumped from the boxcar?"

That was a bright question. Raymond had given me a concussion and I'd been unconscious when the freight pulled into the yards. When the hell was I supposed to have seen him again? But I said, "That's right. I don't even know where it was that he jumped. It couldn't have been too far from the museum, though. He had enough time to get back there on foot, clean out his cottage, and leave town before the police arrived."

Dillard made some notes in a leather-bound book, closed the book, and got out of Lydecker's chair. He said, "I think that will be all for now. We appreciate your cooperation."

"Sure. Are you going to want me to hang around here for a while? Or can I go back to San Francisco today?"

"Is there any particular reason you want to return to San Francisco?"

Another bright question. These FBI guys were pips, all right; if you opened one of them up, what you'd find were wires and gears and little wheels that went round and round in perfect geometric circles. Old J. Edgar had been a technological genius: he'd invented a bunch of functional robots long before the scientists came out with their first experimental model.

I said, "No particular reason, no. It's where I live and where I work, and I'd like to sleep in my own bed tonight. You have my home address and telephone number; that's where I'll be three hours after I leave here."

"Yes, of course," Dillard said. "Well, we'll let you know." And he went out and left me alone again.

I sat there and looked out the window at the parking lot. I still felt tired and my head still hurt. Mild concussion. Christ. But I was lucky I was sitting here and not lying in a hospital bed with my brains half scrambled like a carton of old eggs. For that matter I was lucky I wasn't dead.

Lydecker came in after a while with a statement for me to sign. I asked him if I could go home pretty soon, and he said he thought I could. Then he took me out of his office and put me in another room, a small interrogation cubicle with nothing in it except a table and four chairs. I did some more waiting. At the end of twenty minutes Huddleston showed up with another cup of coffee and the news that the first battery of reporters had arrived outside.

"Terrific," I said. "Do I have to talk to them?"

"That's up to you."

"Then no way. I've had enough questions for one day."

"How's your head?"

"It hurts."

"Want me to get the doc to take another look?"

"No. It's not that bad. Listen, when can I leave? Or am I going to become a permanent fixture around here?"

"You sound a little pissed off," he said.

"Not me. What would I have to be pissed off about?"

"Dillard, for one thing. Those FBI guys are a pain in the ass."

"You said it, I didn't."

He gave me a lopsided grin. He seemed to like me, which was more than I could say for either Dillard or Lydecker; that was some small comfort, at least. I needed all the allies I could get.

"Don't worry," he said, "I think they're going to release you pretty quick."

"I've been hearing that ever since I got here."

"Just hang in a while longer." He went to the door. "Bradford's daughters have both been notified, by the way," he said before he went out. "The chief took care of it while I was out fetching you."

It was another half hour before Huddleston came back; Lydecker was with him. I was in a foul humor by then, but I didn't let them see it. And Lydecker took the edge off it by saying, "All right, we're through with you. You can go now."

"Thanks."

He told me I would be wise to drive straight back to San Francisco, to keep myself available in case I was needed again—the usual speech. I said that was what I intended to do. Huddleston went out front with me and helped me run the gantlet of half a dozen babbling reporters; I tried to ignore them and their questions, but one of them plucked at my bad arm, bringing a cut of pain, and I shook him off and snapped at the pack of them that I had no comment to make. My nerves were in worse shape than I'd thought.

We got outside and over to my car. Huddleston gave me his hand and said, "Good luck," and I said, "I may need it," and got into the car and drove out of there as fast as I could without breaking any laws.

If I could go to my grave without coming back to Oroville again, there was still a chance I'd die a happy man.

It was almost eight o'clock when I drove across the Bay Bridge into San Francisco. The trip had taken me four hours—I had stopped three times, once for gas, once for something to eat, and once for coffee—and I felt lousy. My head throbbed, my thoughts were muzzy, my left arm and hand were sore again. A five-year-old kid with a cap pistol could have tried to mug me and I would not have been able to fend him off.

When I got to my flat I took a beer out of the refrigerator and then went into the bedroom and switched on my answering machine. There were several messages, one of which was from Arleen Bradford and another of which was from Hannah Peterson. Miss A. Bradford said I should call her as soon as I could; she sounded pretty distraught. Her sister said, "This is Hannah Peterson. Please call me right away, it's very important. I need to talk to you about what happened to my father." She sounded distraught, too, even more so than Arleen. Charles Bradford must have meant more to her than I'd given her credit for.

I drank most of the beer as I listened to the playback tape. That was a mistake; I didn't remember until I drained the last of the can that you're not supposed to drink alcohol when you've got a concussion. That one beer had the effect of three or four stiff drinks of hard liquor; I began to feel woozy, light-headed. Arleen Bradford and Hannah Peterson could wait until tomorrow. I was in no shape now to deal with grief or anger or whatever else the two of them wanted to throw at me.

I shut off the machine, shut off the lights, and started to shed my clothes. I had just enough time to get out of my pants before the bed reached up like a hungry lover and gathered me in.

15

Somewhere, a long way off, bells were ringing. I crawled down the steep embankment, trying to get away from the train that was bearing down on me. A guy who looked like Lester Raymond was leaning out of the open door of one of the boxcars, screaming obscenities about death; he smelled like burning flesh. Then he jumped off, and disappeared—poof, like magic stuff—and over the sound of the bells the hobo named Flint said, "You want sympathy? Hey, man, sympathy is what you find in the dictionary between shit and syphillis." Then Raymond was there again, beating my head against something hard and unyielding. Then I woke up.

The ringing bells belonged to the telephone. I fumbled the handset out of its cradle, dropped it, picked it up off the floor, and said, "Yuh?"

"Are you all right?" Kerry's voice said worriedly. "My God, I just saw the morning papers."

"Yuh," I said again. "I'm all right."

"Are you sure? You don't sound all right . . ."

"You woke me up. What time's it?"

"Nine o'clock. The papers said you got a concussion . . ."

"Mild concussion. I'm fine, don't worry."

"Don't worry? You idiot, of course I worry. What is it with you and murder cases? You just get your license back, you get a new client, and bang, here you are all over the news again. And with a concussion besides."

I was awake now. I sat up, wiggled my hips until I had my back braced against the headboard, and ran my free hand over my face; it made a sound like a cat scratching on a door. My head didn't hurt too much, which was a surprise. Neither did my bad arm. I was in great shape, all right. Another couple of days, I thought sourly, and I would be well enough to go out and play a strenuous game of checkers with the other old farts in the park.

"Don't lecture me, okay?" I said. "I can't deal with lectures until I've had my morning coffee."

"One of these days you're going to stay *out* of trouble on a case, and I'm going to be so surprised I won't believe it."

"Did you hear what I said about lectures?"

"You can be so damned exasperating sometimes," she said. "I don't know what to do with you."

"I can think of a couple of things."

"Hah."

"Hey, can I help it if things keep happening to me? If I don't have any luck?"

"No luck? You've got more luck than ten people, or else you wouldn't still be walking around in one piece."

"Nuts," I said. "Did the law get Lester Raymond yet?"

"If they did it was too late to make the papers."

Damn, I thought. Could Raymond pull off the same kind of vanishing act as he had fifteen years ago? The odds were against it. The first time around he'd been as lucky as Kerry claimed I was; this time the FBI would catch up to him before he could go to ground long enough to establish a new identity. It was only a matter of time.

Kerry said, "Are you going to lose your license again?"

"Huh? What makes you ask that? Is there something in the papers?"

"No, there's nothing in the papers. But my God, you just got it back and now this. What if they take it away from you again?"

"They won't do that."

"No? How do you know?"

I didn't know, but I said, "That's what they told me up in Oroville. The FBI and the local cops. They're not holding it against me that Raymond got away."

"Well, if that's what they told you . . ." She sounded relieved, which was more than I could say for myself at the moment. Then, after a couple of seconds of silence, she laughed wryly and without much humor.

I said, "What's funny?"

"Oh, I was just remembering something you said to me the other night. About how you'd never hop a freight, and the closest you intended to get to one was the Oroville hobo jungle. Famous last words. You *did* hop a freight—and you did it just like a bindlestiff."

"Yeah."

"You could have ended up a stiff bindlestiff, too, like the character in Cybil's pulp story, if Lester Raymond had been a little stronger."

"Are we back on the lecture circuit again?"

"Not if I've made my point."

"I got it the first time around. I'm fairly bright that way, you know."

"Sometimes," she said. "How does your head feel?"

"Not too bad today. But the bandage they put on probably needs to be changed. You want to come over and play nurse for a while?"

"That depends."

"On what?"

"On whether or not you've got any ideas about playing doctor."

"Lady," I said, "I don't think I could play doctor today if my life depended on it. My caduceus is out of whack along with everything else; it might be days before it's working again."

She laughed. "Okay, comedian. Go put some coffee on; I'll be there pretty soon."

I got out of bed and doddered into the kitchen and put the coffee on. By the time it was ready, I had taken a quick shower, shaved two days' growth of stubble off my face, and got my pants on. I was just pouring myself a cup when the telephone rang again.

Eberhardt. "I just been reading about you," he said.

"You and everybody else."

In the old days he would have made some smart-ass remark about my penchant for trouble. But the old days were gone. "You okay?" he asked.

"Not too bad, considering."

"FBI give you a hard time?"

"Not really."

"Oroville police?"

"No. I don't think this is going to land me in hot water

with the State Board, Eb. Everybody up there was pretty decent to me."

"Good. Listen, you got some free time this afternoon?"

"I don't know, maybe. Why?"

"I thought you might want to stop over. Shoot the breeze a little."

Uh-oh, I thought. The partnership thing.

"It's kind of lonely around here," he said. "I could use some company. What do you say?"

I wanted to say no; I wanted to say, "Look, Eb, I haven't had time to think about you and me working together, I haven't made up my mind yet." But I couldn't do it. All I said was, "Sure, okay. Early afternoon? Kerry's on her way over this morning . . ."

"Any time you want. I'll be here."

He rang off, and I replaced the handset and sat down on the edge of the bed and sipped my coffee. It's a great life if you don't weaken, I thought. Then I sighed and played back the message tape on the answering machine, so I could write down the telephone number Hannah Peterson had left yesterday. Of the two Bradford sisters, she seemed the easiest to deal with first.

But when I dialed the number, there was no answer. I let it ring a dozen times, just to be sure, before I pushed the button down.

I looked up Arleen Bradford's number in my book, steeled myself, and called her to get that conversation over with. Only she wasn't home either. After three rings there was a click, and her recorded voice said, "This is Miss Arleen Bradford speaking. I am not available at present. Please leave your name and number, and I will return your call."

So I left my name and number, feeling somewhat relieved. Feeling somewhat cynical too. You talk to my machine, I talk to yours. Everything was so damned impersonal these days; machines were taking over. "Hello. This is John Doe's computer calling to hire your computer to investigate Jane Smith's computer. Click. Whirr. Clang."

I took my coffee back into the kitchen. There were some eggs and a package of bacon in the fridge; I cooked up some of each, and sat down to eat them. And then the downstairs door buzzer went off.

I thought it was Kerry; she had a key, but sometimes she rang the bell anyway from force of habit. I went out and punched the button that released the foyer door lock, without bothering to ask through the intercom who it was. Then I opened the door and waited for her to come up the stairs.

But it wasn't Kerry who appeared in the hallway moments later. It was Jeanne Emerson.

I blinked at her, standing there in my undershirt with my belly hanging over the waistband of my pants. I sucked it in as she approached, for all the good that did; I still felt fat and old and sloppy. She was dressed in a pair of slacks and a tank top that did nice things for her breasts, and she had a big portfolio case in one hand. Her black hair glistened as if she had rubbed it with some kind of oil. The fragrance that came from her as she approached was spicy and exotic, full of Oriental mystery—or so my nose and my hot little brain imagined.

"I was hoping you'd be home," she said, smiling in a grave sort of way. "Do you mind my stopping by?"

"Uh, no," I said. "Not at all."

"I wasn't sure if I should, after what happened to you in Oroville. I probably should have called first, but . . ."

"No, it's all right."

"May I come in?"

"Sure. Sure thing."

I stepped aside and she brushed past me; that spicy perfume or whatever it was tickled my nose again and put funny thoughts into my head. When I turned to shut the door I saw her wince. She was staring at the back of my skull where they'd shaved off some of the hair and stuck the bandage on.

"It's not as bad as it looks," I said.

"I hope not. Do you have much pain?"

"Not really."

"That's good." She studied me speculatively for a moment. Then she smiled again, a different kind of smile this time. "Do you know what a sin-eater is?" she asked.

"Huh?"

"A sin-eater. A person who takes on the sins of others, absorbs them for purposes of absolution. It's an old Cornish superstition."

"Is that what you think I am? A sin-eater?"

"In a way," she said. "But it's not the sins of the individual you keep taking on; it's the sins of the world. In microcosm, of course."

She's kidding me, I thought. Or is she? In any case, she was making me feel self-conscious. Here I was, standing around in my underwear thinking dirty thoughts, and she was nominating me for sainthood again.

"Well, uh," I said, and stopped because I couldn't think of anything to say. Then I was aware again of the portfolio she was carrying. "What have you got in there?" I asked her, not very brightly.

"Oh, yes—some photos I did for a piece on secondhand bookstores a couple of years ago. They'll give you an idea of the sort of thing I want to do with your pulps." She was looking at the shelves of them as she spoke. "That *is* an impressive collection," she said.

"Well, I've been at it a long time."

She opened the portfolio and took out a handful of eight-by-ten glossies and put them on the coffee table. "These are black-and-white," she said. "I was going to do a black-and-white study, but all those bright colors are wonderful. Color would be much better."

She went to the nearest of the shelves and I waddled over there after her; if I'd had a tail it probably would have been wagging. I watched her take down one of the pulps that I'd arranged so their covers faced into the room, slip it out of its protective plastic bag, and study it.

"This is fantastic," she said. "I didn't know they had covers like this."

What she was holding was an early issue of *Dime Mystery* with cover art that depicted three half-naked young girls tied up in a room full of red firelight, an old hag with a gnarled cane and an evil leer, and a drooling Neanderthal type, whose name was probably Igor, dragging another attractive young victim into the lair. The issue's featured stories were "Murder Dyed Their Lips" by Norvell W. Page and "Slaves of the Holocaust" by Paul Ernst.

"It's typical of the shudder pulps back in the thirties," I told her.

"Shudder pulps?"

"Also known as weird menace pulps. Sex-and-sadism stuff, though pretty mild by today's standards."

"Are women always treated so shabbily in these magazines?"

"The torture stuff? Pretty much, I'm afraid."

She put the copy back on the shelf. "Then that's something I'll want to touch on in the article. Contrast the attitudes of the thirties with those of today."

I said, "About that article, Ms. Emerson . . ."

"Jeanne. Now don't tell me you're going to say no."

"Well . . ."

She stepped closer to me and put her hand on my arm and looked up into my face. It was an imploring look, but there was intimacy in it, too. That and the nearness of her and that damned musky perfume were enough to start me drooling like old Igor on the pulp cover.

And so of course the door opened and Kerry walked in.

She'd used her key; and she'd done it quietly enough so that neither Jeanne Emerson nor I had heard it in the latch. She started to sing out a hello, stopped dead when she saw us. Jeanne let go of my arm and backed up a step. I just stood there like a dolt.

The three of us looked at one another. The expression on Kerry's face said: What's *she* doing here? The expression on Jeanne Emerson's face said the same thing. Christ only knew what the expression on my face said.

Nobody spoke for what seemed like a long time. Then I said, "Uh," and "Uh" again, and finally found some words to go with the grunts: "Kerry, this is Jeanne Emerson. She's a photojournalist, she wants to do a piece on me . . ."

"I'm sure she does," Kerry said.

"She just dropped by to show me some photos . . ."

"Mm. How do you do, Ms. Emerson?"

"Fine, thanks. And you? Kerry, is it?"

"Kerry Wade. I'm just dandy."

They smiled at each other in that overly pleasant, calculating way women have in situations like this. It made me nervous. I wanted to say something else, but anything I was liable to toss out between them would only make matters worse. I kept my mouth shut.

Kerry said at length, "We were going to have breakfast. Won't you join us, Ms. Emerson?"

"No, thanks. I've already had my breakfast. Some other time, perhaps."

"I'm sure I'd enjoy it."

"I'm sure I would, too." Jeanne went to the coffee table and scooped up her portfolio case. "I'll leave these glossies here for you to look at," she said to me. "In a day or two I'll call you and we'll set a time to begin shooting."

"Well, uh . . ."

"Good-bye, Ms. Wade," she said to Kerry. "Nice meeting you."

"The same here, Ms. Emerson."

When she was gone, Kerry looked at me for a time without saying anything. I felt like a kid who'd been caught with his hand in the cookie jar. Except that I hadn't been. Thinking about something doesn't mean you intend to do anything about it.

"She came by unexpectedly," I said. "What could I do? Tell her not to come in?"

"Did I say anything?"

"No. I'm just trying to explain . . ."

"Why do you think you have to explain?"

"Kerry, I told you before about Jeanne Emerson. I told you about that magazine article she wants to do . . ."

"You didn't tell me you were such good friends."

"We're not good friends."

"It looked like you were getting to be when I came in."

"Nuts," I said. "Let's not talk about Jeanne Emerson, okay? Let's have breakfast."

So we had breakfast and we didn't talk about Jeanne Emerson. We didn't talk about much of anything. Kerry was as overly pleasant to me as she'd been to Jeanne, which meant that there was a storm of unknown magnitude brewing inside her. I wished she would let it come out; I wished she would cloud up and rain all over me, as they used to say. But that didn't happen. All I got was the saccharine and the moody silence.

Over coffee in the living room, I said, "Eberhardt called after you did; he wants me to stop over for a while this afternoon. Why don't you come along? That'll keep him from pestering me about the partnership thing."

"Oh goody, I like to be useful."

"I didn't mean it that way. I just meant—ah Christ. Look, we won't stay long, and afterward we can go for a drive or something. . . ."

"I don't think so," she said. "I've got some work to do this afternoon that I've been putting off."

"But—"

"I'll just change your bandage and be on my way."

What could I say? There wasn't anything you could say to her when she was in one of her moods; all I could do was weather it until it passed.

Twenty minutes later, I was alone with a new bandage on my skull and a new headache inside it. I looked at the four walls for a while. Then I sighed and put on a shirt, put on a coat, and went out and got into my car.

And the old sin-eater headed over to Eberhardt's place to scarf up some more sin on his long and wearying journey into sainthood.

16

Eberhardt lived in Noe Valley, in an old two-storied house that had belonged to a bootlegger during Prohibition. Or so Eberhardt had told me once; he'd had a lot of beer at the time and he might have been putting me on. He'd lived there for nearly three decades, since a few months after his marriage to Dana. And he had almost died there six weeks ago.

I found a place to park in front and went up onto the porch and rang the bell. It took him a while to answer the door, and when he did I was struck again by how much he'd changed since the bribe thing and the shooting. There was so much gray in his hair now that it looked as though it had been dusted with snow. His face, once a smooth, chiseled mixture of sharp angles and blunt planes, had a slackness to it—the beginnings of an old man's jowliness—that made him look a dozen years older than he was. He had lost weight, too, at least fifteen pounds; he looked bony and gaunt, and the slacks and pullover he wore hung on him like old clothes on a scarecrow. When I'd asked him about the weight loss the last time I stopped by he'd tried to make a joke out of it by saying, "It's nothing, I just been off my feed a little lately." But that was pretty much the way it was. He just wasn't eating the way he should, if he was eating much at all.

"Sorry I took so long," he said. "I was on the phone."

"Anybody important?"

"No," he said. "It was Dana."

I went inside and he shut the door. This was the living room, where the shooting had happened; Eb had got it right in front of the door, and I had been scorched when I came running in through the swing door from the kitchen. He'd put throw rugs over the carpet where the two of us had lain, because the rug-cleaning people hadn't been able to get out all of the bloodstains. He was going to buy a new carpet one of these days, he'd told me, as soon as he could afford it.

The room, the memories of that Sunday afternoon and its aftermath, made me feel uneasy all over again. I had been here four times since the shooting—it had been the same each time. I wondered if Eberhardt was plagued by the same specters, and if he was, how he could go on living here with them. And with the ghosts of his dead marriage.

I said, "Dana called? How come?"

"Her sister's husband had a heart attack, he's in intensive care over in Marin General. She thought I'd want to know. Hell, what for? My ex-brother-in-law's an asshole; we never got along. I never heard a word out of him or Dana's sister the whole time *I* was in the frigging hospital."

I had nothing to say.

"She didn't sound too good," Eberhardt said. "Dana, I mean. And not just because of the heart attack. I think she's having trouble with her boyfriend."

Dana was living with a Stanford University law professor in Palo Alto. The professor may have been the reason she'd left Eb, or he may have come into her life afterward; in any event, she'd told me in the hospital right after the gun job that she loved him.

I said, "Why do you think that? She didn't say anything along those lines, did she?"

"No. But she wanted to talk; and she did some hinting around." He made a bitter noise that was not quite a laugh. "Could be she'll want to come crawling back one of these days."

I wasn't so sure about that. Dana was proud, stubborn, and independent; she was not the kind to come crawling back if her relationship ended. But I said, "Would you take her back?"

"Hell, no. I'd kick her out on her ass."

"I thought you still cared for her . . ."

"Not any more. I hate her guts."

He'd changed inside, too, that was the thing. He was harder now, colder, emptier. The toughness used to be tempered by compassion, but every time I talked to him these days I got the feeling he no longer cared about anybody, not even himself. Dana was part of it, but the biggest part was that bribe. He'd lost his self-respect, and he was floundering around in a sewer of guilt and shame and self-pity.

But maybe I could haul him out. Give him a sense of purpose again; give him back his self-respect. Give him the partnership . . .

You're not Eberhardt's keeper, Kerry had said to me. And *You didn't have anything to do with him being where he is now.* And *Isn't what you want the important thing?* She was right on all three counts. She also didn't think it would work out; she was likely right about that too. What was the sense in giving Eberhardt the partnership if it didn't do either of us any good?

Back and forth, back and forth. Make up your mind,

damn it, I thought. Why can't you make up your mind?

We went into the kitchen. Eberhardt said, "You thirsty? I got some beer in the box."

"I guess I could use one."

He opened the refrigerator and took out a couple of bottles of Henry Weinhard's. "I'm not supposed to drink anything alcoholic yet," he said. "Bad for my insides, the doc says, because they're still on the mend. The hell with him, too."

"It's your funeral, Eb."

"Damn right it is." He gave me one of the bottles, twisted the cap off his. "Let's go out in the yard. Not too much sun lately; might as well take advantage of it while we got it."

It was a small yard, enclosed by a board fence, with a Japanese elm and a barbecue pit and some bushes and a couple of pieces of outdoor furniture. We'd been out here just before the shooting, drinking beer, talking, getting ready to cook a couple of steaks; it made me faintly uneasy to be back in the yard, too.

We sat on the outdoor furniture and drank our beers and talked about nothing much for a while. Then Eberhardt asked me about Charles Bradford and Lester Raymond, so I told him the way it had been—all the details, the stuff that hadn't got into the papers.

When I was done he said, "You're a hell of a detective; I always said that. But your problem is, you don't know when to quit."

"I've been a cop too long, I guess. I always want to know all the answers."

"You need somebody to keep an eye on you," he said. "Before you get killed or thrown in jail. Or they take your license away permanently."

"Eb . . ."

"Yeah, I know. I'm pushing about you taking me into your agency. And you haven't decided yet, right?"

"Not yet, no."

He leaned forward in his chair. "Listen," he said, "all I want is a chance. Just a chance. I'll go nuts if I sit around here doing nothing much longer."

"What about one of the bigger agencies? You could hook up with the Pinks, with your background. They'd have more for you to do, you'd make more money . . ."

"Yeah, pulling crappy guard duty somewhere. I don't want that kind of job."

"What do you think it's been like for me the past twenty years, Eb? A lot of hard, mostly crappy work, no glamour, and damned little money. I barely made enough to get by when things were going good."

"I told you before, I can bring in some business."

"But would it be enough to support both of us? These are tough times, you know that. I don't see that they're going to get much better either."

"If you're going to say no," he said, "go ahead and say it. I won't hold it against you."

The hell he wouldn't. I could see that in the hard, bitter shine of his eyes. "I'm not going to say no yet; I'm not ready to say anything yet. Give me a few more days, will you?"

"Sure. A few more days. But I got to have something to do pretty soon or I'll start climbing the goddamn walls."

Silence settled between us. But it was not the good companionable silence of the old days; it was strained, like that between two strangers.

I broke it finally by saying, "There's an American League playoff game on TV. You feel like watching it?"

"Nah. Greedy jocks, greedy owners, stupid announcers—who the hell cares about professional sports these days? Not me, that's for sure."

"Yeah."

"You don't have to hang around, you know," he said. "You probably got a hot date with Kerry coming up anyway."

"Sure," I lied. "That's right."

"Call me when you make up your mind," he said, without looking at me. "I won't bug you again, meanwhile."

There wasn't anything more for me to say. I nodded, gripped his shoulder, and left him sitting there in his lawn chair staring at something only he could see.

I was in a low mood when I got back to my flat, and ten minutes on the telephone shoved it all the way to the bottom. Kerry was the first person I called, to see if she wanted to have dinner with me; she said no, she was still working and she didn't feel much like company tonight. She sounded grumpy, so I asked, "Are you still miffed about Jeanne Emerson?" and she said, "Don't be silly." But then she said, "Why don't you go have dinner with her? I'm sure she could whip up an Oriental delicacy or two for you." After which she muttered something about talking to me later and rang off.

So then I called Hannah Peterson's number in Sonoma; she still wasn't home. But Arleen Bradford was, and in a pretty emotional state. The first thing she said to me was, "It's all your fault," in a shrill, angry voice. "Why did you have to let Lester Raymond get away? Why couldn't you have gone to the police?"

"Look, Miss Bradford—"

"He murdered my father!" She almost shouted the words, so that I had to pull the receiver away from my ear.

"The police will get him," I said. "He's not going to—"

"I won't pay you any more money. You hear me? I won't pay you another cent after what you did!"

And bang, she slammed the receiver down in my ear.

I sighed, went out of the bedroom, turned on the TV, and tried to watch the baseball game for a while. But nothing much was going on, and when one of the announcers said in response to a fielding error, "He gets paid a million dollars a year to catch popflies like that," I got up in disgust and shut the thing off.

I drove down to Union Street and bought myself an anchovy-and-pepperoni pizza for dinner. But by the time I drove back up the hill, found a parking place, and walked to my flat, the pizza was cold. I put it into the oven to warm it up, left it in too long, and burned the crust. Then I discovered I was out of beer.

It was one of those days, all right. And there was only one way to deal with days like that.

I took two aspirin for my headache and went to bed with a hot pulp.

The telephone jarred me out of sleep on Sunday morning, just as it had on Saturday morning. The nightstand clock said a few minutes past nine. It wasn't anybody I knew this time; a youngish-sounding male voice gave his name as Harry Runquist and then said, "I'm Hannah Peterson's fiancé. I'm calling from Sonoma."

I said, stifling a yawn, "What can I do for you, Mr. Runquist?"

"Do you know where Hannah is? You're the last person I can think of who might know."

"Where she is?"

"Because if you do, you've got to tell me. I've been half out of my head worrying about her."

There was a kind of controlled desperation in his voice; it made him sound hoarse. And it woke me all the way up. "I don't know where Mrs. Peterson is," I said. "I've only talked to her once and that was three days ago. How long has she been missing?"

"Since Friday night."

"Have you tried calling her sister?"

"I tried calling everybody," Runquist said. "Nobody's seen her, nobody knows where she might be. I even went to the police last night. They said you had to wait forty-eight hours before you could file a missing-person report. I tried to tell them about her father, about this son of a bitch Raymond, but they wouldn't listen."

"What about Raymond?"

"They said they hadn't had any reports of him being in this area; they said I was worrying about nothing—she was upset about her father and she probably just went off somewhere to be by herself. But they don't know Hannah. She wouldn't do that, not without telling me."

"Are you saying you think Lester Raymond might be responsible for her disappearance?"

"No. I don't know. There's just no other reason I can think of for her vanishing like this."

I remembered the telephone message I'd had from Hannah Peterson on Friday night. She had sounded pretty distraught, all right, almost pleading—and maybe frightened. But of Lester Raymond? It just didn't make sense that he would try to harm one of Charles Bradford's daughters.

"You're a detective," Runquist said. "Maybe you could find her, find out what's going on. I want to hire you."

"Well, I'm not sure that I—"

"I love Hannah, mister," he said, and his voice had dropped to a tense, gravelly whisper, like a man coming down with laryngitis. "I'm wild about her. And I don't know what else to do. Somebody's got to do something. Come up here and talk to me about it, will you? I'll pay you whatever you want. Only for God's sake help me find her!"

What can you say to that kind of emotional plea? Only one thing, if you're somebody like me.

"All right, Mr. Runquist," I said. "I'll come up and talk to you. I'll see what I can do."

17

It was a little better than an hour's drive to Sonoma, forty miles northeast of San Francisco, and my watch said eleven-fifteen when I got to the big, tree-shaded plaza in the middle of town. It's a pretty place, Sonoma, located at the lower end of the Valley of the Moon and surrounded by wooded hills, orchards, farmland, and vast acres of vineyards. Although the wines of the Napa Valley to the east are more prominent, a lot of people who know about such things say that the Sonoma Valley produces wines of equal if not superior stature. There are a trio of wineries within the city limits of Sonoma, in fact, one of which, Buena Vista, has the distinction of being the first winery in California; it was founded in 1832 by a Hungarian named Agoston Haraszthy, who selected and imported thousands of cuttings from the finest vineyards of Europe and who was responsible for creating the type of wine called zinfandel. I knew all of that because I had spent a fair amount of time up here over the years. If I ever moved out of the city, which wasn't likely, Sonoma was the place I would come to.

I turned right in front of the city hall. As early as it was, there were a lot of people out and around—picnickers in the plaza, the inevitable tourists wandering around gawking at the place where California's independence from Mexico had been declared in 1846 and at the Mission San Francisco Solano de Sonoma, and the other old frame and adobe brick buildings that flanked the square. Church bells echoed in the distance. The air was warm and heavy with the smell of growing things and, faintly, of pulped grapes: this was the time of year the crush takes place. All in all, a pleasant small-town Sunday morning. Except that Harry Runquist wasn't enjoying it, and Hannah Peterson, wherever she was, probably wasn't either. And for a parcel of reasons, neither was I.

Runquist had told me he lived on East Napa Street, half a dozen blocks from the plaza. I found the place within a couple of minutes: a big, old, twenties Victorian with a lot of gingerbready trim on the front porch and windows that had leaded-glass borders. The number, 618, was plainly visible on one of the fancy porch columns. A huge carob tree shaded both the front lawn and a realty company's FOR SALE sign jutting up near the sidewalk.

I made a U-turn at the next corner and came back and parked in front of the house. When I got up on the porch I saw that there was a pumpkin sitting on a table to one side; even though Halloween was still better than three weeks away, it had already been carved into a jack-o'-lantern. There was a screen door, with the main door behind it standing wide open. From somewhere inside I could hear a steady clacking, clattering sound—the kind a toy or model train makes.

I pushed the doorbell button. The train sound quit almost immediately, and a few seconds later a guy materialized in the dark hall within and looked out at me through the screen. I said, "Mr. Runquist?" and he said, "Yes," and unlatched the screen.

He was in his mid-thirties, medium height, medium build, with a lot of curly brown hair and a saturnine face that was homely in a pleasant sort of way—the kind of face women like because it has strong masculine characteristics. But there were deep hollows in the cheeks now, and beard stubble flecking them, and his eyes were bloodshot. He'd been drinking—I could smell wine on his breath—but he was sober and pretty strung out. He couldn't seem to keep his hands still.

"Thanks for coming," he said. "You made good time."

"Traffic wasn't bad for a change."

"Come on in."

The room he led me into was smallish and had probably been referred to as "the front parlor" fifty years ago. It was a comfortable room: old heavy furniture, a tiled Victorian fireplace, built-in shelves laden with books, and rattan blinds drawn over windows in the front and side walls. An archway to the left opened into what had been intended as a dining room; now, though, it was empty of furnishings and contained only a massive model train layout. The model had been built on sheets of plywood that took up most of the carpet in there—an intricate configuration of tracks, dozens of miniature cars and locomotives, depots, loading platforms, crossing signs, lighted signal lamps, semaphores, a bunch of other scale-model accessories, and a bank of control switches.

Runquist saw me looking at the layout and said dully, "O-gauge stuff: American Flyer, Ives, Lionel . . . you know anything about model railroads?"

"No, I'm afraid not," I said. "I heard you running it when I came up."

"It helps keep my mind occupied."

"Are you in the railroad business, Mr. Runquist?"

"No," he said. "I'm a winemaker—Vineland Winery, up near Glen Ellen. My grandfather founded it. Model railroading's just a hobby." He passed a hand across his face. "Hannah's a train buff, too. That's how we got together. Met at a party, found out we were both buffs . . . she helped me build part of the layout."

I nodded, remembering what Hannah Peterson had told me about her father's passion for trains rubbing off on her. "Have you known Mrs. Peterson long?" I asked him.

"Almost a year." He glanced at one of the chairs, started toward it as if he intended to sit down. Then he changed his mind and pawed at his face again. "I could use a glass of wine," he said. "Would you like one?"

"It's a little early for me, thanks."

"Me, too, usually. But I've been so damned worried about Hannah. . . . Come on, we'll talk in the kitchen."

I followed him out into a big, old-fashioned kitchen bright with morning sunshine. A rear porch opened off of it; it had been made over into a kind of dining area, with a long table set under windows that overlooked the back yard. The yard contained a walnut tree, a pepper tree, and plenty of shrubs; and near the back fence was something I hadn't seen in years—a shake-roofed gazebo.

"Nice place you've got here," I said as Runquist opened the refrigerator.

"Yeah," he said. "Too big for me, though."

"You live here alone, do you?"

"Ever since my divorce two years ago." He took out a bottle of white wine, poured some into a glass, put the bottle away again. "My ex-wife got custody of our daughter; took Monica back east to live with her mother. I got the house."

He sounded bitter about it. But it was none of my business, so I didn't say anything. I was thinking about the jack-o'-lantern on the front porch. Runquist must have carved it for himself, for some sort of nostalgic reason; that, coupled with the model train layout, told me a good deal about what kind of man he was. I already knew what kind of woman Hannah Peterson was, or thought I did, and I wondered if he had made a mistake falling in love with her. She had doubtless made a lot of men unhappy in her life, men who saw only her beauty and her superficial charm. Because I found myself liking Runquist, I hoped he wasn't going to be just another name on the list.

He drank some of his wine, moved restlessly to one of the windows and stood looking out into the yard. "Too many memories here," he said, half to himself. "I should have moved out long ago."

"Is that why you've got the house up for sale?"

"Part of the reason. Hannah's selling her place, too.

We bought some land up in the mountains east of Glen Ellen and we're building a house on it. We're going to be married when it's finished."

"Oh," I said, "I see."

He nodded. "We've both had offers since we put the houses on the market, but they've been too low. Things in real estate are tight right now—" He broke off. "To hell with real estate," he said. "It's Hannah we should be talking about."

"When was the last time you saw her, Mr. Runquist?"

"Friday evening, at her house. She called me at the winery that afternoon, after the Oroville police notified her of her father's death, and I went over to be with her. She was pretty upset. She'd never been close to her dad, but finding out he'd been murdered . . . that hit her hard."

"It's a hell of a thing, all right."

"She told me about seeing you, trying to convince you not to go up there hunting for him. Maybe you should have listened to her; maybe it would have been better for all of us if you'd stayed out of Oroville."

There was no censure in his voice, only anguish. He wasn't blaming me. If she'd told him she thought I was a homosexual it did not seem to matter to him. And if that was the case I liked him for his tolerance, too.

I said, "Her father would still be dead, even if I'd stayed away. And Raymond would have got away with murder a second time."

"I know," Runquist said. "But Christ, what if Raymond *did* come down here after Hannah? What if he's responsible for her disappearance? What if . . ." He didn't finish the sentence, but I knew what he was thinking. He tilted his wine glass again; his hand was a little unsteady.

"I still don't see how that's possible," I said. "What reason could Raymond have for harming Mrs. Peterson?"

"I don't know. All I know is, she's missing and she shouldn't be."

"How long did you stay with her on Friday?"

"Until about six o'clock."

"Why did you leave her then?"

"I had a meeting scheduled here at my house; I'm chairman of the committee for this year's Sonoma Wine Festival. I wanted to cancel it, but Hannah said no, she'd be all right." He turned from the window and began to pace. "The meeting broke up about eight o'clock. I was just about to telephone Hannah, but she beat me to it. She said she'd had a call and she had to go out, but her car was out of gas. That's happened to her before; she's always forgetting to fill up when she's low. She knows I keep a five-gallon can in my garage and she wanted me to bring it over."

"Did you?"

"Yes. Right away."

"How did she seem?"

"Even more upset than earlier. Frantic, almost. She said she had to be somewhere and she was already late."

"That's not much to get frantic over."

"I know. I tried to get her to tell me where she had to go, who she was seeing, but she wouldn't say. Hannah can be . . . well, she can be stubborn sometimes."

Yeah, I thought, I'll bet. "I don't suppose she said anything about the phone call either?"

"No. As soon as I poured the gas into her tank, she drove off." He frowned, as if he'd just remembered something. "There was a sleeping bag in the back seat," he said.

"Sleeping bag?"

"Yes. I noticed it just before she drove away. She's not the kind to go out camping, not Hannah. It must have belonged to her late husband. But what was she doing with it in her car?"

I shook my head; there was nothing to be gained by trying to answer questions like that. "Was that the last time you saw or spoke to her?"

"The last time, yes."

I pulled one of the chairs out from the table and straddled it with my arms resting on its back. "She called me, too, on Friday night," I said, "and left a message on my answering machine. I don't know what time—she didn't say—but it had to have been before eight-thirty. That was when I got home from Oroville and checked the machine."

Runquist quit pacing. "Why would she call you? You live in San Francisco; how could you do anything for her that I couldn't?"

Another rhetorical question. I said, "All she said was that she wanted me to get in touch with her right away and that it was important."

"Did you try to call her that night?"

"No. I was tired and I thought it was only that she was upset about her father. I called twice yesterday; no answer either time."

Runquist finished his wine, went immediately to the refrigerator and emptied the bottle into his glass, and started to work on that.

I asked him, "Are you sure Mrs. Peterson hasn't been home since Friday night?"

"Not positive, no. But I called again at ten-thirty that night and she wasn't there. I should have gone over and waited for her but I didn't. I didn't go to her place until yesterday morning, after I tried calling twice more and still didn't get an answer."

"You have a key to her house?"

"Yes. We're engaged, I told you that."

"I'm just asking, Mr. Runquist."

"Her bed hadn't been slept in," he said.

"Was everything in order inside the house?"

"As far as I could tell, it was."

"Did you check to see if any of her clothes or other belongings were missing?"

"Yes," he said. "Everything was still there. Her suitcases, too—I made sure of that."

"What did you do then?"

"Talked to her neighbors. None of them had seen her. Then I came back here and called everyone I could think of that she knows; none of them had seen or talked to her either. That was when I started to get scared. I even drove up to the house we're building in the mountains. When she still hadn't turned up by six o'clock I went to the police. I told you on the phone what they said."

"Did you check her house again this morning?"

"Before I called you," he said. "Her bed still hadn't been slept in, and nothing had been touched."

I got up from the chair. "It might be a good idea if I had a look at the house," I said. "Would you mind going over there with me, letting me in?"

"No, of course not. Anything you want."

He finished his wine, plunked the glass down on the table, and led me out to the front porch. The jack-o'-lantern grinned at us from the table—an incongruity in the bright Sunday morning sunshine. It made me think, in spite of myself, of witches and goblins and things that went bump on dark nights.

18

Hannah Peterson's house was on Lovall Valley Road, out near the Buena Vista Winery. It was a modern ranch-style surrounded by a redwood fence, with plenty of lawn in front, an attached two-car garage, and a swimming pool glinting at the rear. On one side were acres of gold and scarlet grape vines stretching off into the distance; on the other side was a fenced pasture with a couple of horses grazing in it. A FOR SALE sign similar to the one at Runquist's place was imbedded in the middle of the lawn.

I parked in the driveway, and Runquist and I got out and went over onto a porch studded with old oak wine barrels that had been turned into planters for ferns and other decorative plants. He used his key to unlock the front door. "Hannah!" he called as we stepped inside. "Hannah!" But his voice echoed emptily in the stillness.

Runquist took me from room to room. As he'd said earlier, nothing was out of order; the place, in fact, was immaculate—the kind of house I had never felt comfortable in because there was no personality to it, no sense of the individual who occupied it. Swedish Modern furniture, carpeting and drapes and accessories that complimented it perfectly; pictures hung just so, ashtrays and lamps and vases arranged just so, the tile and fixtures in the kitchen and bathrooms gleaming. No books or magazines anywhere; people who don't read always put me off a little. It was like walking through a museum exhibit. The only thing that gave any indication that I was in a house belonging to Hannah Peterson was a huge, impressionistic painting of an ancient steam train that hung in the family room at the rear.

I opened closet and cabinet doors at random, with Runquist's tacit consent. I did not expect to find anything, and I didn't. The closets and cabinets were as clean and neat as the rest of the place.

In the master bedroom, the spread over the bed was rumpled and pulled down at one corner; that was the only thing I had noticed anywhere that was out of place. I asked Runquist, "How do you know Mrs. Peterson didn't sleep here the past two nights? Was the bed like this on Friday?"

"Yes. She was lying down when I got here; that's how the spread got pulled around like that. If she'd slept here either night she'd have made the bed when she got up. She's compulsive that way."

We started back to the front room. "Mrs. Peterson's

late husband left her this house, is that right?" I asked.

"Right. Joe Peterson. He built it for her."

"Built it himself, you mean?"

"Yes. He was in the construction business."

"Did you know him?"

"Only by name. He died three years ago. Heart attack; he was twenty-five years older than Hannah."

We reentered the living room. I said, "You told me you talked to the neighbors yesterday. Just the immediate neighbors or what?"

"Everybody who lives within a block of here. There aren't that many; this is almost the country out here. None of them saw her at any time on Friday night."

"Does she normally park her car in the driveway?"

"No. Inside the garage."

I nodded, and he moved away from me in that restless way of his and started a turn around the immaculate living room. Only it wasn't quite as immaculate as I'd first thought; I noticed now, as Runquist paced in front of the fireplace, that in the middle of the hearth there was a small pile of ashes and charred paper overlain with cigarette butts. The rest of the bricks in there had been swept clean.

I went over and knelt down and poked through the pile. Some of the pieces of paper were not completely charred; they were glossy—like the remains of photographs that had been torn up and then set afire. I fished out the largest of the unburnt pieces. It was the bottom third of a color snapshot, showing the legs of a man and a woman and an expanse of lawn or meadow.

Runquist had come over beside me. I straightened and held the fragment out so he could see it. "Do you know what this is?"

"Part of a photograph," he said.

"Sure. But what I'm asking is, why would Mrs. Peterson tear up and burn a bunch of photos?"

"I don't know."

"You weren't here when she did it?"

"No."

"Were these remains here on Friday afternoon?"

"I don't remember," Runquist said. "Why? You think it means something?"

"Maybe. People don't normally destroy photographs this way; and not on the same day they've learned of a death in the family, unless they have a pretty good reason for it. Any idea what this snap might have been of?"

He shook his head. "I don't think it's anything I've ever seen before."

"Does Mrs. Peterson have a photograph album? Or a box or something where she keeps photos?"

"If she does she never showed it to me."

"Where does she keep her personal papers and things?"

"I don't . . . wait, yes I do. The sitting room—she uses that as an office."

The sitting room was off the master bedroom. It was smallish, with not much in it except for a sofa, a reading lamp, an antique console radio, and a trestle desk set against the wall next to a curtained window. I said, "I'll need your permission to look through the desk."

"Go ahead."

I opened each of the drawers. Pens and pencils and other paraphernalia, notepaper, envelopes, file folders crammed with paid bills and receipts and canceled checks—but no photographs of any kind. I turned away from the desk. In one wall were a pair of sliding mahogany doors; I pushed one of them open and looked into a closet full of cardboard packing boxes, small cartons of stationery supplies, odds and ends. And on top of one of the packing boxes, two thick leather-bound photo albums.

I carried the albums over to the desk. Runquist stood peering over my shoulder as I opened one and began leafing through the pages. The pictures were all family-type snaps, most in color and nearly all of Hannah Peterson at various ages up to about sixteen, doing the various things that kids do to get their pictures taken. An older girl who had to be Arleen Bradford was in some of the photos; Charles Bradford was in a couple more; and a faded-looking blond woman with nondescript features was in half a dozen of the early ones. Bradford's wife, probably. I wondered what had happened to her. Neither Arleen nor Hannah had mentioned their mother, as if she had never really been an important part of their lives. Or of their father's.

The second album was much more interesting. The first few pages were all Hannah, of course; she had to be something of a narcissist to have collected all these photos of herself. Not that that was surprising; I had met the lady, after all. Two pages of Hannah at her high-school senior prom where she had evidently been the belle of the ball, judging from the number of boys hanging around her. A page of Hannah in cap-and-gown at her graduation ceremony, and another page of Hannah in a bikini at some lake, with more boys paying homage. And then four pages of nothing but those little paper corners you use to keep photographs in place in an album, some stuck to the pages and some lying loose as if the photos they'd held had been ripped out.

I turned another page. A couple of snaps had been pulled off there, too, and of the ones remaining, one was lying at an angle near the bottom, a corner of it bent as though the album had been closed on it. A photo Hannah had meant to burn and overlooked? I picked it up and studied it.

Color shot of a teenage Hannah standing alone on the bank of a wide river, one hand on her hip, giving either the camera or whoever had taken the picture a provocative look. I turned it over. On the back, in red ink in a fancy feminine hand, was written "Me in Nebraska."

There was something about that notation that started

vague stirrings in my memory, like ripples on placid water. I handed the snapshot to Runquist. "Does this mean anything to you?"

"Nebraska," he said. "That's where Hannah lived with her first husband."

"Oh? Where in Nebraska?"

"Omaha, I think."

"What was his name, do you know?"

"Adams. I can't remember his first name. She doesn't talk about him much; I don't think their split was very friendly."

"Why do you say that?"

"Well, she did mention once that they fought a lot. He was more than twenty years older, like Joe Peterson was; I don't know why she kept taking up with older men." He pawed at his face again. "She also said something once about having to sneak away when she finally decided to leave him. He wouldn't have let her go if she hadn't, she said."

"So she was afraid of him?"

"I think she was, yeah."

Omaha . . .

I flipped through the rest of the album. There were no other photos of Hannah or anybody else in Nebraska; that had evidently been the batch she'd destroyed. The rest of the photos included several men. I asked Runquist if he'd ever seen a picture of Hannah's first husband, this Adams.

"No," he said.

"So you wouldn't know if any of these guys might be him?"

"No. She never showed me any of these photos."

Omaha. Omaha, Nebraska . . .

Then I had it, the connection, and I said, "Jesus Christ!" before I could check myself. Because there was a jolt in it; there was a hell of a jolt in it.

Runquist said, "What's the matter?"

"Nothing. Just an idea."

"What sort of idea?"

I couldn't look at him; he'd have seen it in my expression. I caught up the two albums, took them back to the closet and shut them away. By the time I turned around again, I had my facial muscles under control.

"Listen," I said, "I'm going to go talk to the neighbors again; there might have been somebody you missed. Suppose you stay here, in case she comes back. Or calls."

"All right."

"While you're waiting you can write me out a list of names and addresses of Mrs. Peterson's friends in this area. I know you talked to all of them yourself, but I want to check with them again. Will you do that?"

"Sure, whatever you want."

I got out of there; went over past the fenced pasture where the horses were grazing, toward a big white house on the other side. My mind kept working, putting it all together, making me sweat a little. I did not want to believe it was possible, but there it was.

Hannah Peterson's first husband hadn't been anybody called Adams. His name had been Lester Raymond.

She had been married to the man who had murdered her father.

19

It *had* to be that way. Arleen Bradford had told me that Hannah had run off to Nebraska with her first husband; that she'd done it not long after Raymond murdered his wife and her lover and disappeared with all the cash and negotiable securities; and that Raymond was the macho type and used to come over to the Bradford place fairly often. Hannah had only been eighteen at the time, a young and impressionable age, and she'd inherited her father's love of trains; another train buff like Raymond was just the type to attract her. Add all of that together with the fact Raymond had lived in Omaha himself for thirteen months in 1967 and 1968, and you had too many things that dovetailed too perfectly to be coincidence.

The irony of it was bitter. Raymond had gone berserk when he found out about his wife's infidelity, but he'd been playing around himself; some macho men were like that, the old double standard. Or, hell, maybe he hadn't gone berserk after all. Maybe he'd known about the cash and securities, maybe he'd gone out to the architect's place in Malibu with the intention of stealing the money, maybe the murders had been premeditated. So he could afford to go off with his young girlfriend, Hannah, and start a new life.

In any case, where did Hannah herself fit in? Had she been a party to the killings and the theft? It wasn't likely, not from what I knew about her. She may have had questionable morals, but she wasn't a cold-blooded killer. Whatever had motivated Raymond that afternoon in Malibu, I doubted if she had found out what he'd done until afterward.

Why had she stayed with him once she *did* find out? A combination of reasons, probably. Fear; Runquist had said she'd been afraid of the man. Fear of the law, too, of being put in jail as an accessory to homicide. Her youth. Love for Raymond, or at least a strong infatuation. Maybe a sense of adventure and excitement at the idea of living with a fugitive. And the money, of course. Yeah, money would have been a strong mitigating factor in anything Hannah had ever decided to do.

Then why had she finally left him? Again, a combination of reasons. Disillusionment. Raymond was a lot older than she was, he was basically a law-abiding, hard-working citizen; he'd taken most of the money and put it into a house and a business in Omaha. Hannah wasn't ready to settle down as the wife of a middle-aged man in Nebraska. So they'd fought, and the relationship had deteriorated, and finally she'd got up enough courage to sneak out one night and come running back home to California.

But why home? Well, neither her father nor her sister knew the man she'd run off with was Raymond; they probably hadn't known she was in Omaha either until she told them. So there was no danger to her there. Still, hadn't she been afraid Raymond would come after her, for fear that she might expose him to the police? No, it wouldn't work that way. She couldn't have exposed Raymond without exposing herself as an accessory; Hannah was no martyr, and Raymond had to have known that as well as anybody. Maybe she'd written him a note, or called him once she was clear of Omaha. If he left her alone she'd never tell anyone about him, all she wanted was her freedom . . . something like that.

And Raymond *hadn't* chased after her. What he'd done instead was to cover himself, just in case Hannah slipped up, by moving out of Nebraska and heading for Denver. That had all been late in 1968. Meanwhile Hannah had taken up with the rock musician and was busily engaged in forgetting about Lester Raymond. Except for those photos in her album, that is. For some reason—narcissism again, maybe—she'd kept four pages of snapshots of her and Raymond and Omaha for her own private viewing.

It was easy enough to figure why she'd burned the photos on Friday night: after all these years Lester Raymond had come back into her life, and in the craziest, most terrifying way possible. No wonder she'd been distraught. It wasn't just that her father had been murdered; it was that he'd been murdered by her former husband. Rage, or whatever emotion had been governing her at the time, had led her to rip the photos out of the album and destroy them.

And then what?

Sometime between six o'clock, when Runquist left her, and eight o'clock, when she'd telephoned him, she had had another call. From Raymond? Yeah, it must have been. But why would he have contacted her of all people?

Well, I thought then, why not? He was on the run again, with a fresh murder rap hanging over him; he didn't have much money this time, he had no transportation; he was desperate. And when the story broke in the papers on Friday, Hannah's name had been right there—"Hannah Peterson, of Sonoma." She was the *only* person he could turn to for help, because he could force her to give it to him; he had her in a box on the accessory thing back in 1967. If she refused to help him—with money, a car, a place to hide, whatever—he'd tell the police all about her involvement.

But that was as far as I could take it on deduction and speculation alone. Where had Raymond called Hannah from on Friday night? Here in Sonoma? It didn't have to be; he could have holed up anywhere in the vicinity, told her to come pick him up or bring him something. Why had she called me? And where were the two of them now? Had Raymond done something to her? Or was it just that she was on the road somewhere, with or without him, maybe on her way back home?

I hadn't told Runquist about any of this; the shape he was in, it would have pushed him right over the edge. The last thing I needed on my hands right now was a candidate for the twitch bin. Telling the police about it was another matter. I had to do that, and I would—but not just yet. The problem was, even with all my fancy deduction and speculation I didn't have one shred of proof to back it up. Hannah had burned the photographs; none of her family or friends knew much about her first husband; the FBI obviously hadn't identified her yet as the woman Raymond was married to in Omaha; and at first consideration the whole idea sounded screwy as hell. By the time I got done talking to the Sonoma cops, the county cops, the FBI, and Christ knew who else, it would be tomorrow afternoon.

Maybe I could turn up a lead on my own, here and now. If I could manage that I would have something more substantial to take to the authorities. I'd give myself the afternoon, until five o'clock. If I hadn't come up with anything by then, and if Hannah still hadn't returned home, it was straight to the Sonoma Police Department. . . .

One of the horses in the pasture made a loud snorting noise. It came from close by and it jarred me out of my musing. I had stopped walking and was leaning up against the fence, and the horse, a big reddish beast with hairy legs, was giving me a baleful look from about five feet away. Its teeth were bared as if it were thinking about taking a bite out of my neck.

I backed off in a hurry, started toward the big white house again. The sun was past its zenith now, beating down on the top of my sore head. Past noon. Less than five hours. Not much time, even if I had had anything specific to work with.

Hannah, I thought, where did you go on Friday night?

Where the hell did you go?

The woman who answered the door at the big white house hadn't seen Hannah Peterson in several days, she said. What did I want with Hannah, anyway? I told her I was a friend of Harry Runquist's and that it was a personal matter. She said, "Humpf," and gave me a sour look; it was plain that she neither liked nor approved of Hannah. I chalked it up to female jealousy. The woman was forty and frumpy, with hair that poked up from her skull like a cluster of steel springs out of a torn mattress.

But I not only got the same negative response to my

questions from half a dozen other neighbors over the next thirty minutes, I also got the same sense of disapproval or dislike or both. And two of the people I talked to were men. One matronly type referred to Hannah as "that woman"; one of the men, who was about sixty, assumed a righteous air and clacked his dentures and said he wouldn't be surprised if she'd chased off to a motel with some man. He sounded a little envious just the same.

So Hannah wasn't popular with her neighbors. So what? She was a walking advertisement for sex. Most women would resent her for that, and most men would covet her either openly or behind proper facades. She also had plenty of money, inherited from a husband twenty-five years her senior, and she probably hadn't worked a day in her life. Not many people would like her much, I thought, and those that did would be poor love-sick bastards like Runquist or carbon copies of Hannah herself—sybaritic, money-hungry types with things in their past that they never mentioned to anyone.

I had covered all of the houses within two blocks of Hannah's place to the west, and within a block and a half to the east. There was one more left to try on the east side, to make it two blocks both ways; if I drew a blank there as well, there didn't seem to be much point in going any farther.

It was a small cottage set well back from the street inside a wood-and-wire fence. The front yard was lush with a variety of fruit trees—apple, peach, plum—and rows of pea and bean and tomato vines, plus a watermelon patch, a squash patch, and bunches of artichoke and swiss chard plants. It looked like one of those deluxe Victory Gardens FDR kept urging people to plant during the Second World War. In the middle of it, a stooped, skinny guy in his seventies was industriously whacking away at the ground with a hoe. Behind him, on the porch, a round little woman about the same age was sitting in the shade, drinking something out of a glass and watching him. The two of them seemed content with their respective roles—him working, her watching.

I went up to the front gate. "Excuse me, sir," I called to the guy. "I wonder if I could talk to you for a minute."

He quit hoeing, squinted at me for a couple of seconds, and apparently decided I looked respectable enough to deal with. He started in my direction. There was a lot of bounce in his step; he may have been old in years, but he had some spark left.

"What can I do for you?" he said when he got to the gate.

"I'm trying to locate a woman named Hannah Peterson," I said. "She—"

"Who?"

"Hannah Peterson. She lives a couple of blocks down that way"—I gestured—"in the house with vineyards on one side and the horse pasture on the other."

"Oh, her," he said, and grinned. He glanced over his shoulder at the round woman on the porch. Then he winked at me. "The blonde with the big tits," he said.

"Uh-huh. Right."

"Well? What do you want with her?"

"I'm a friend of the man she's engaged to. Harry Runquist. He's pretty worried about her; she's been missing since Friday night."

"She has? Missing, you say?"

"Yes. I was wondering if maybe you'd seen her sometime Friday evening. Or any time since."

"Saw her yesterday morning," he said. "So how could she be missing since Friday night? Don't make any sense."

"Are you sure it was yesterday morning you saw her?"

"Sure I'm sure," he said. "I may be old, but I ain't senile. I know one day from another."

"What time yesterday morning?"

"Around nine o'clock. I was on my way to the grocery.

Edna—that's my wife—needed some milk." He frowned. "Ain't got a cow," he said regretfully.

"Where was it you saw Mrs. Peterson?"

"Inside her garage."

"You mean the garage door was open when you drove by?"

"That's what I mean."

"What was she doing?"

"Looked like she'd been loading something into her car," he said. "Trunk was up."

"Was she alone?"

"Not exactly. Another car'd just pulled into the driveway. Company, I reckon."

"Did you see who was in it?"

"Nope. I was too busy looking at the blonde's tits." He winked at me again. "Man never gets too old to look at a nice set of tits."

"Had you ever seen the car before?"

"Which car?"

"Not Mrs. Peterson's; the other one."

"Can't say that I had, no."

"Do you remember what kind it was?"

"Hell, I don't know nothing about cars," he said. "They all look alike to me. Just a car, that's all."

"New, or an older model?"

"More new than old, I guess."

"What color?"

"Green. Dark green."

"So you drove on past," I said, "and went to the store. How long was it before you came back?"

He shrugged. "Twenty minutes, give or take."

"Was the dark green car still in Mrs. Peterson's driveway?"

"Nope."

"How about Mrs. Peterson's car?"

"I dunno. Garage door was down."

"Did you see any sign of her?"

"Nope. And believe me, son, I was looking. Tits like she's got . . ." He sighed, glanced back at his wife again, sighed a second time, and said, "Sure must be nice," in the same regretful voice he'd used when he said he didn't have a cow.

I thanked him and started back toward Hannah's house. I thought I could take his story pretty much at face value; he was a long way from being senile, and he hadn't struck me as the type to make up stories. And if it *was* the truth, then Hannah Peterson hadn't disappeared Friday night but sometime yesterday.

But that fact only clouded the issue even more. Why hadn't her bed been slept in Friday night? Why, if she'd stayed away all night, had she come back to her house yesterday morning? To load something into her car, maybe—but what? And who had been in the other car, the dark green one?

20

When I got back to Hannah's house I rang the doorbell and Runquist let me in. He'd found some wine here, too; there was a big glass of it, red this time, in his left hand.

"No calls, nothing," he said. He gave me a painfully hopeful look. "You find out anything?"

"Maybe. But I don't know yet what it means."

I repeated the gist of my conversation with the elderly

neighbor. But I still kept my speculations about Hannah and Lester Raymond to myself.

"I don't get it," Runquist said. He sounded even more bewildered and worried than before. The wine was starting to get to him; you could see it in the glaze of his eyes. "If she was all right yesterday morning, why didn't she call me? And where was she Friday night?"

More rhetorical questions, just like the ones I'd been asking myself. I said, "Do any of Mrs. Peterson's friends drive a dark green, late-model car?"

He shook his head as if to clear it and paced around for fifteen seconds or so. Then he said, "No. None of them I know own a green car. Who the devil . . ."

"Just take it easy, Mr. Runquist. Do you mind if we go out into the garage?"

"The garage? What for?"

"I want to take a look around."

There was an entrance to the garage off the kitchen. Most of the floor space was empty and swept as clean as the interior of the house; there weren't even any oil spots on the cement. I wandered around with Runquist at my heels. Washer-and-dryer combination, a small stack of firewood, some pieces of lawn furniture, a workbench that looked as though it hadn't been used in a long time, and not much else. From what was in here now, I couldn't even begin to guess what Hannah might have been loading into her car yesterday morning.

"What kind of car does Mrs. Peterson drive?" I asked.

"Toyota Tercel," Runquist said.

"What year?"

"This year. She's only had it a few months."

"What color?"

"A sort of beige."

"Do you know the license plate?"

"I think so. . . . Seven-three-five NNY."

I jotted that down in the notebook I carry. While I was

doing that I remembered what he'd told me earlier about driving over here Friday night to put gas in Hannah's empty tank. I asked him if the five-gallon can had been full or if he'd put in less than that amount.

"Less," he said. "I emptied the can, but there couldn't have been much more than a gallon in it."

"So she'd have had to stop somewhere pretty soon and fill up."

"That's what I told her just before she drove off."

"Is there any particular gas station she goes to?"

He frowned. "Not that I can think of, no."

"Does she prefer to pay cash for things like gas? Or does she use credit cards?"

"Plastic," he said. "Always."

"Which oil company cards does she have?"

"Mobil, Chevron . . . I think that's all."

Which meant that she'd probably gone to either a Mobil or Chevron station on Friday night. There couldn't be that many of either in Sonoma or its outlying areas; if I could find the right one it might at least tell me which direction she'd been heading. I had nothing else to work on at the moment, no other angle. The dark-green car appeared to be a dead-end.

I said, "Did you write out that list of names and addresses of Mrs. Peterson's friends I asked you for?"

"Yes. It's inside."

We reentered the house and Runquist went and got a sheet of notepaper from an end table next to the sofa. When he gave it to me I saw that there were eight names, seven of them women, all but two with Sonoma addresses; one of the two lived in Glen Ellen, the second in Napa. I folded the paper into thirds and put it into the inside pocket of my jacket.

Runquist asked, "What now?"

"I go to work. Do you want me to drop you back at your house?"

"Yeah. Everywhere I look here, I see Hannah."

He drank the last of his wine, glanced around the room, and then said, "I'd better take this glass into the kitchen. Hannah doesn't like dirty dishes sitting around the living room."

He went out with the glass, and I thought: You poor bastard, you. Hannah Peterson had him so wrapped up he'd have crawled naked through the plaza if she'd asked him to. For his sake, I hoped she loved him just half as much as he loved her; that it wasn't just his money and an interest in his winery she was after. For his sake, I hoped she was all right and came home safe and sound from wherever she was.

Runquist came back from the kitchen pretty soon and I followed him outside and waited while he locked up again. His movements were a little unsteady and he had some trouble getting his key into the deadbolt latch; I thought that he'd probably taken another shot of the red wine while he was in the kitchen. But I didn't say anything to him about it. It was none of my business how he got through this, or how anybody got through a crisis except me.

I let him off in front of his house, listened to him urge me twice to call right away if there was anything he should know, wrote down his phone number in my notebook, and watched him make his way across the lawn. His shoulders were slumped; you could almost see the weight of the thing pressing down on him.

Up on the porch, the jack-o'-lantern grinned its idiot grin as he mounted the steps and I drove away.

It took me an hour and twenty minutes, five abortive stops, and a small piece of luck to find the filling station Hannah Peterson had stopped at on Friday evening.

It was a Chevron station on the Sonoma Highway—Highway 12—just outside the city limits to the north, not much more than a mile and a half from where she lived. But I'd gone south first, the direction that led to Napa and San Francisco, and that was why it was so long before I got around to the right place. But it was a good thing I'd done it that way. The guy who had waited on her that night had Sundays off, but he'd just dropped by for a few minutes to shoot the breeze with the attendant on duty; he was there when I drove in, and within earshot when I asked the kid who came to the car about Hannah.

"Sure," he said, "I remember her." He cracked thick, grease-blackened knuckles; he was that kind of guy. "She come in must of been about nine. A fox. Yeah, a real fox. But spacey, you know what I mean?"

"Upset. Strung out."

"Right." He cracked his knuckles again. "I thought maybe she was on something. Kept mutterin' to herself, havin' a regular old conversation like there was somebody else in the car with her."

"What was she saying?"

"I dunno. Lot of gibberish to me."

"Can you remember any of it?"

"Well . . . one thing she said a couple of times, didn't make no sense. Sounded like 'bundles of stuff.'"

"Bundles of stuff."

"Yeah. Or maybe bundlestuff, like it was one word."

I repeated that too: "Bundlestuff." Then another, similar word popped into my mind and I said, "Wait a minute. Bindlestiff. Could the word have been bindlestiff?"

"Could of, yeah," the knuckle-cracker said. He gave me a dubious look. "That supposed to mean something?"

"I don't know yet. Can you remember anything else she said?"

"Nah. I wasn't payin' much attention. A fox, sure, but spacey; you never know with them spacey chicks, I had one pull a gun on me once. Just bundlestuff or whatever the hell. While I'm washin' the windshield. 'It's got to be bundlestuff,' she says."

"Like that? 'It's got to be bindlestiff'?"

"Yeah, come to think of it. Just like that."

"Thanks."

"Sure. Say, how come you're askin' about that blond fox, anyhow?"

"That was no blond fox," I said, "that was my wife."

He didn't get it; all he got was the wife part. He backed off a step. "Hey, man, I didn't mean no offense . . ."

"None taken," I said, and gave him a sour grin, and went over to where a public telephone booth stood at the edge of the station apron.

Inside, I found a dime in my pocket and dialed Runquist's number. He picked up immediately, as if he'd been sitting there waiting to pounce on the thing. He said, "Hello?" twice, and when I told him who was calling he said, "Oh," in a low voice; he'd wanted badly for it to be Hannah. But then he said, "What is it? What've you found out?" and he still sounded hopeful. He also sounded more sober than he had when I'd left him: he'd had enough sense to lay off any more wine.

"I'm not sure yet," I said. "Does the word 'bindlestiff' mean anything to you?"

"Bindlestiff?"

"It's an old-fashioned term for hobo—"

"I know what it means. Why are you asking about bindlestiff?"

"Because I found the service station Mrs. Peterson stopped at on Friday night. The attendant who waited on her said she was muttering something to herself about bindlestiff."

"The house we're building," Runquist said.

"Pardon?"

"That's our pet name for it, the new place up in the mountains. Bindlestiff Manor."

"I don't see the connection."

"There *isn't* any connection. Except that we're both

railroad buffs. We were up at the house site one day and Hannah made a joke about how it was too bad freight trains didn't run through the mountains because that way it would be easy for her father to visit us. I said, then all the other hoboes would want to stop here, too, and we'd have to call the place Bindlestiff Manor."

Cute, I thought. The old man's riding the rails, living in hobo jungles and drinking cheap wine, because he can't find a job; and his affluent daughter is not only building a fancy house up in the mountains, not only trying to stiff him out of his share of the family inheritance, but is also making jokes at his expense. Real cute.

"But why would she go up there by herself on Friday night?" Runquist was saying. "The house isn't finished; there isn't any electricity or plumbing. And she wouldn't have spent the night there—not Hannah."

Maybe she wouldn't, I thought, at least not by choice, but Lester Raymond might have. Runquist seemed to have forgotten the sleeping bag in her car; I hadn't. Suppose Raymond had demanded she find him a place to hide temporarily, over the weekend? *It's got to be Bindlestiff* . . .

"It could be a dead-end, Mr. Runquist," I said. "The attendant here might have misunderstood her. But I'll take a look at the house just the same."

"But I drove up there yesterday; I told you that. There wasn't any sign of her."

"You looked inside the house?"

"I didn't go all the way in, no. I didn't see any need to; her car wasn't there."

"I still want to take a look around. Unless you have some objection . . ."

"No. God, no. I'm just trying . . . I don't know what I'm trying to do. Go ahead, do whatever you think best."

"How do I get to the place?"

He told me. It wasn't more than fifteen miles from where I was now and it didn't sound too difficult to find; I knew the area a little, and his directions were simple enough so that I didn't even need to write them down.

"Listen," Runquist said after a couple of seconds' pause, "if she did go up there Friday night, do you think it was because of Lester Raymond?"

"I don't know."

"But if it was, then . . ."

I did not want to get into it with him; I did not want to have to lie to him. I said, "I'll call you again later, Mr. Runquist," and rang off.

21

I drove north on Highway 12, through Boyes Hot Springs and Fetters Springs and Agua Caliente—places all well-known around the turn of the century for their mineral baths. Vineyards and low wooded hills took over beyond there; the autumnal reds and golds of the grape vines glistened in the afternoon sun like frozen fire.

Pretty soon the turnoff for the rustic little village of Glen Ellen appeared. Glen Ellen was where Jack London had lived the last years of his life—Jack London, the most famous of all the literary figures who had ridden the rails in their youth, the champion of road kids and gay cats and bindlestiffs. I remembered Arleen Bradford telling me that her father's favorite book had been *The Road,* London's collection of autobiographical essays on his hoboing days. Funny how trains and hoboes kept running through this whole business with the Bradford family and Lester Raymond, interwining now and then, like a peculiar leitmotif. And there was something a little dark and unsettling about it, too, something I did not want to dwell on at the moment.

A couple of hundred yards beyond the Glen Ellen turnoff, I noticed a sign at the edge of a private road that said: VINELAND WINERY • PREMIUM SONOMA VALLEY WINES • TASTING ROOM. Runquist's place. I could see it as I passed by, an old brick building coated with ivy, nestled back in a grove of trees with the vineyards stretching away at the rear.

The turnoff I wanted was a mile or so farther on. Trinity Road. The only road you could take from the Valley of the Moon to the Napa Valley across the Mayacamas Mountains that divided the two—a distance of maybe fifteen miles, I knew, because I had driven it a couple of times in the past. The mountains were heavily wooded, dotted with occasional small vineyards over toward the Napa side, and offered some spectacular views of one valley or the other, depending on which end of the road you were on. So naturally people with money had begun building secluded homes up there several years back; a lot more were being built even in these economically depressed times by people like Hannah Peterson and Harry Runquist.

Trinity Road, a narrow two-laner, began to wind upward almost immediately after I made the turn off Highway 12. There were some switchbacks in it, too, because the ascent was so steep and rapid. I had gone less than a mile when the vista began to open up on my right and behind me as I climbed. It was pretty spectacular, all right. The vineyards, the little villages here and there, and in the distance, rising dark against the sky, the Sonoma Mountains that bounded the valley to the west.

I pretty much had Trinity Road to myself. There weren't any other cars going in my direction, and I only passed one heading the other way. I kept one eye on the odometer, because Runquist had told me the house he and Hannah were building, or rather the lane that led to it, was exactly 3.2 miles from the Highway 12 intersection. It was the only private road within several hundred yards, he'd said. And to make sure I didn't miss it, there was a whitewashed gate between two mossy old stone cairns at the foot of it.

I had no trouble; I saw the lane and the gate and the stone cairns as soon as the odometer clicked off 3.2 miles. I slowed, swung over onto it, stopped in front of the gate. Fir and oak trees grew dense and in close to both Trinity Road and the lane here; all I could see ahead and on either side was a narrow ribbon of crushed gravel that curled away to the left, then vanished into the woods.

When I got out and went over to the gate I found that it wasn't locked, just fastened with a spring-type latch. I swung it open; drove through and kept on along the lane. There was not much point in reclosing the gate while I was on the property.

The lane hooked through the trees for maybe a hundred yards before it emerged into a good-sized clearing. The far left-hand side of the clearing fell away into a long slope covered with chaparral and scrub pine; that was where the house was being built. It was not difficult to understand why Hannah and Runquist had picked this spot. There was a mostly unobstructed view of the valley from Kenwood on the north to El Verano on the south.

I parked on the near side of the house. It was almost half-finished and bigger than the kind you usually saw up in the mountains. Hannah would have insisted on that, I thought, for show, if for no other reason. The side deck was a good twenty feet wide and jutted out over the slope on steel support girders; the railing for it hadn't been built yet. The back half of the place was still an open mini-forest of vertical beams. On the grassy earth in front and alongside were stacks of two-by-twos and two-by-fours, sheets of plywood, roofing shingles, bricks, and other building materials.

There wasn't anything else to see from where I was, no sign of anybody or that anybody had been here recently other than the construction people. After a few seconds I got out into a light mountain breeze that carried the smells of pine and chaparral and cut lumber. Some bees made buzzing noises in a patch of clover nearby; birds chattered at each other in the trees. Otherwise, the clearing was wrapped in that soft kind of stillness you only find in the country.

I went over to the rear of the house, up onto the deck. The floor was empty except for a handful of forgotten nails; equally empty were the unfinished rooms inside. I made my way through the forest of beams anyway, past the skeleton of a massive fireplace and into the roofed-over front section. Most of the walls were up in there, and another fireplace was nearing completion in what was probably the master bedroom. A stack of bricks and a wooden mortar tray were on the floor in front of the hearth.

So was a quilted nylon sleeping bag. And a paper bag that had come from Jack in the Box. And an empty half-pint bottle of sour-mash whiskey.

Those things erased any doubt that Hannah Peterson had come up here on Friday night. And it looked as though she hadn't been alone when she got here; she wasn't the type to eat fast-food or to drink sour mash straight out of a bottle. Or, as Runquist had said, to spend the night in a sleeping bag in an unfinished house. Unless she was forced to, I thought. *Had* she spent the night here with Raymond? There was only the one sleeping bag. Well, if she had slept with him she'd done it under duress and it amounted to rape. Whatever else she was, she wasn't enough of a cold-hearted bitch to willingly sleep with the man who'd just murdered her father.

The sleeping bag was zippered all the way open and

folded back; I could see without touching it that there wasn't anything inside. I sat on my haunches and used thumbs and forefingers to open the paper sack. It contained what I'd expected it to—the remains of a fast-food supper. From the feel of the lone french fry, it had been there a while.

I straightened and took a turn around the room. There wasn't anything else to find in there; or in any of the remaining rooms. The way it seemed, Raymond had spent Friday night here, with or without Hannah, and then beat it sometime yesterday. But Hannah had been back at her place in Sonoma at nine A.M.; if Raymond was the one in the dark-green car that had pulled into her driveway, where and how had he got the car? And what was he doing at her house? And what had Hannah been loading into her Toyota?

I didn't like the way things were shaping up. It had all appeared to be coming together, and maybe it still was, but I was beginning to get a sense of twists and turns and hidden hazards, like a bad road on a dark night with a bridge down somewhere up ahead.

Outside again, I went around to the other side of the house. More building materials; a lightweight aluminum roofer's ladder leaning against the wall; one of those portable outhouses you see nowadays on construction sites. Across thirty yards of grassy open space, at the edge of another patch of woods, were a tumbledown shed and what was left of an old stone well. The shed and the well, and those ancient, moss-caked cairns down at the foot of the lane, told me somebody else had lived on this property before Hannah and Runquist purchased it. But not in a good long while, judging from the condition of that shed. There had probably been a house here, too, that had had to be razed before they could start putting up the new one.

Another lane, or a continuation of the one from Trinity Road, cut through the trees over there; from where I stood I couldn't see where it led to. I looked at it for a few seconds. Then I crossed to the edge of the clearing and looked at it some more, closer up.

What I saw deepened my growing sense of uneasiness. This lane hadn't been used much; its surface was all but obliterated by a thick carpeting of pine needles and oak leaves and rotting humus. But there were faint parallel marks in the carpet now, as if a car had gone along there recently. A clump of tall grass that grew at the clearing's rim had been crushed, too, and the soft earth underneath showed the clear imprint of a tire tread.

Maybe one of the builders had driven over here for some reason, I thought. Except that the imprint was narrow and fairly shallow, not the kind a heavy vehicle like a pickup truck or van would make. It was the tread of a passenger car's tire, and a small passenger car at that.

I went along the lane, walking in the middle, listening to the bird sounds and the dry brittle cracking of the leaves and needles underfoot. Feeling a slow gathering of tension across my neck and shoulders. The lane made a sharp dogleg to the left after twenty yards, extended another twenty after that, and petered out at a massed jumble of decayed boards and creepers and shrubs that rose up at the base of a sheer rock wall. It had once been a building of some kind—a small barn, maybe, or a chicken coop—but that had been long ago.

To the left there were not many bushes, just a lot of grass that grew thick and knee-high. The two parallel tracks that hooked through it, around to the rear, were plainly visible. I knew what I was going to find as soon as I saw those tracks, and when I got around behind the decayed building I found it: a car parked nose up to a blighted live oak, half-hidden there in the grass—a beige Toyota Tercel, license plate 735-NNY. Hannah Peterson's car.

The windows were all rolled up; I bent to peer through the one in the driver's door first, then the one in the rear door. The interior was empty, nothing at all on the seats or the floor or the dashboard or the rear-window deck. But the keys were still hanging from the ignition slot.

I got out my handkerchief, wrapped it around my right hand, and tried the driver's door. It wasn't locked. I leaned in and punched the button to open the glove compartment. A map of Sonoma County, a map of California, a plastic envelope containing the car's registration and owner's manual, two unopened packages of Marlboro cigarettes, and a small flashlight. I shut the compartment, looked around in front and back another time without finding anything. Then, still using the handkerchief, I slid the keys out of the ignition and went around to the rear and opened the trunk.

On the deck inside was a rifle partially wrapped in an old blanket, a small carton that contained a wood-handled revolver and boxes of cartridges for both it and the rifle, and a larger carton full of neatly folded clothing. The rifle, I saw when I pushed aside part of the blanket, was a bolt-action center-fire Savage—the kind hunters use for deer and larger game. The revolver was a Smith & Wesson .38 hammerless, a belly gun. The clothing in the bigger box was all men's stuff, shirts and pants and lightweight jackets; on top, like some sort of crown, was an old railroader's cap.

Now I knew what Hannah Peterson had been loading into the trunk yesterday morning. And I had a pretty good idea why, too. The guns had probably belonged to her late husband; the clothes had either belonged to him or they were her father's and she'd been storing them. Raymond was a fugitive and a multiple killer, and even though he'd likely beat it out of Oroville with his own gun, it made sense he'd have wanted more weapons and ammunition. Getting them from Hannah was a lot safer than stealing them. The same was true of fresh clothing; whoever the items in that carton had belonged to, he had been the same approximate size as Raymond.

But what was it all still doing in the trunk? And why had the car been driven back here and hidden this way? And by whom?

I shut the trunk lid, put the keys back into the ignition, closed the driver's door. There were no other sections of crushed or bent grass in the area; the person who'd driven the car in here had walked back out along the wheel tracks, without detouring anywhere. I went back that way myself, around to the other side of the collapsed building. There wasn't anything to find over there, no tracks of any kind. The Toyota had been brought here and abandoned—that was all.

Okay, I thought. The rest of it was up to the police and the FBI. I'd done all I could without overstepping myself again; and I had dug up enough circumstantial evidence of a link between Hannah Peterson and Lester Raymond, or at least that *something* fishy was going on, to stir up official interest.

I hurried back along the lane. When I reached the clearing I started across it at an angle toward the front of the house.

And that was when I noticed the blood.

It was a few yards away on my right, a sun-streaked blob of it that shone a dull red-brown against the bright chlorophyll green of the grass. I had seen too much blood in my life not to recognize it, even from a distance. Ah Jesus, I thought, Jesus. I veered over there and bent down to examine it. A big splotch, dry and dark and flaky to the touch; it had been there a while, but not too long—a day or so. Animal blood, maybe. Only it wasn't animal blood; I felt that down deep where the gut feelings, the bad feelings, always come from. It was human blood and somebody had spilled a lot of it here yesterday. Too much for any kind of superficial wound.

The tension, now, was like a hand clutching the back of my neck. I could feel the pain of it the length of my bad left arm, and in the tender bruised place on my scalp. Straightening, I began to walk a slow, widening spiral outward away from the splotch. The second bloodstain, smaller than the first, was ten feet to the west. The third, smaller still, was back to the north. The fourth and fifth lay in that direction, too, forming an irregular and grisly trail.

And where the trail led was straight to the old stone well.

It had been long abandoned, that well. If it had ever had a windlass of any kind it was gone now; there was nothing above ground except a foot or so of its circular shaft with a wooden lip cemented on top. Two wooden covers, like halved circles, had been built to fit over the lip, but neither was in place; they had been dragged off and were lying on the ground nearby. On the near side of the lip was a small thin smear of dried blood.

I leaned over to look inside the well. But the overhanging tree branches blotted out the sun, and it was too dark in there for me to make out much except for the gleam of water. I trotted around to my car, taking care to avoid the bloodstains in the grass, and unhooked the heavy-duty flashlight from its clip under the dash. But when I got back to the well and aimed the light down inside I still couldn't see much. There was water in it, all right, maybe a dozen feet below ground level—scummy and brown, its surface scabbed with dead leaves—but nothing else was visible, and there was no way of telling from up here how deep the water was.

Leave it to the cops, I thought. Let them fish around and find out what's in there. What could you do anyway? Tie a rope around yourself and one of the trees and climb down inside like some sort of screwball Tarzan?

But I did not want to go away from here without knowing what was in the well. I *had* to know, damn it. I splashed the light around the sides. The well had been built of rough-edged fieldstone, caked now with moss, and the diameter of the shaft was about four feet. No handholds. No ladder of any kind . . .

Ladder, I thought.

I shut off the flash and crossed to the house, to where the lightweight aluminum ladder I had noticed earlier was propped. It was a ten-footer, and at the top was a pair of those metal hooks so that the ladder could be anchored for use on steep roofs. I carried it back to the well and lowered it inside. The wooden lip surmounting the outer rim was narrow enough for the hooks to fit over: the ladder hung straight and steady against the inner wall. The lip seemed strong enough to support my weight, and when I tested it by swinging over and standing on one of the ladder's upper rungs, it proved out that way.

There was one more thing I needed, and I went and hunted it up from the building materials near the house—a cut piece of two-by-two about five feet long. I took that back to the well, swung over onto the ladder again, and began to climb down. I did it slowly, a rung at a time, with the length of wood in my left hand, the flashlight in my pocket, and my right hand wrapped tight on the ladder.

The smell in there was bad down near the water, dank and fetid. It was cold, too, colder than you'd expect only a few feet below ground. I could feel myself sweating from the tension, the sweat turning clammy in the cold darkness. I made myself breathe through my mouth.

When I got to the bottom rung I was only a couple of feet above the scummy surface of the water. Carefully I eased my body around until I was facing away from the ladder. Then I clamped the two-by-two under my arm, maneuvered the flash out and switched it on. Opposite and below to my right, one of the stones jutted out a little; I stretched my right leg down there and anchored my shoe against the projection. It was an awkward stance—one foot on the stone, one foot and one hand on the ladder—but it was stable enough so that I could put the flash away again, take the two-by-two in my left hand, and reach down to probe the water.

The first thing I discovered was that it was no more than three feet deep. The board went down that far and thunked against a solid floor, which meant that the well had been filled in with more rocks or maybe cement and the stagnant water was what had seeped in during the last rain. I started to stir around with the wood—and almost immediately it bumped against a heavy yielding mass that shifted sluggishly under the water.

I tried to snag it, to hoist it up to the surface. But my left arm was weakening from all the exertion, and I couldn't seem to get any purchase. I shifted the two-by-two over to my right hand and wedged my hips back against the ladder so that I would not have to hold on with the left hand. The sweat was in my eyes now, stinging; I swiped it away before I probed again with the wood.

This time I managed to catch it on some part of the underwater mass. And when I heaved up and back, the thing down there bobbed into shadowy view and I was looking into white staring eyes like peeled eggs, at matted blond hair and a bloated face that had once been pretty.

Hannah Peterson.

My stomach turned over; I had to tighten the muscles in my throat to keep from gagging. I jerked the two-by-two back to release it from the jacket she wore, to let the body sink again. When it pulled free it sliced through the water and struck something else—another heavy yielding mass directly under the ladder.

Christ! I worked the wood down there, in movements that were a little agitated now, thinking: It can't be *another* corpse; how could it be? But it was. The board caught in clothing again and up it came for me to stare at in disbelief.

The second body was that of Lester Raymond.

I was still staring when there was a sudden violent jerk on the ladder from up above. It was so violent and so unexpected that I had no chance to brace myself. My right foot slipped off the projection of stone; I dropped the length of wood and tried to twist around to clutch at the ladder, but it jerked again and that dislodged my left foot. I yelled, flailing with my arms—and in the next second I was in the water, half-submerged, struggling wildly to get my head out so I could breathe. Some of the foul stuff poured into my mouth, funneled into my throat; I retched it up. It was fifteen seconds or so before I got my legs down and my head up, and when I blinked my eyes clear and peered upward, all I saw was rough stone, blue sky, tree branches. The ladder was gone.

Somebody had shaken me off deliberately and then pulled it out. Somebody had trapped me down here in three feet of stagnant water with a pair of corpses.

22

For the first few seconds I felt an unreasoning panic fueled by revulsion and sudden claustrophobia. There was a scream building in my throat; I struggled to keep it there, because if I let it out it would be surrendering to the panic. I opened my mouth wide and forced myself to breathe deeply, evenly. I forced myself to stand still, too, with my arms splayed out and my hands flat against the stones on either side. The wildness went out of me in slow swirls, like water down a clogged drain, but when it was gone I had myself under control again.

One of the bodies brushed against my leg, and I shuddered and backed up until my hips touched the wall. The water came to just above my waist. Something cold and clammy was pressed to my lower jaw; when I realized that and pawed it off I saw that it was a decay-blackened oak leaf. I tilted my head back. There was still nothing in the circular opening above except sky and the overhanging tree branches.

Quiet up there, too. Even the birds had quit their chattering. The person who had left me to drown or die of starvation would be headed off the property by now—the same person who had killed Hannah Peterson and Lester Raymond and dumped their bodies down here. Returned to the scene of the crime, probably to do something about Hannah's Toyota back there by the collapsed building. Spotted me, hid in the woods until I climbed down inside here, and then slipped up and grabbed the ladder. Dead men tell no tales. But I wasn't dead yet, and when I got out of here I would tell plenty of tales because I had a pretty good idea who that person had to be.

If I got out of here . . .

The back of my head had begun to throb and burn; some of the stagnant water had got in under the bandage and irritated the wound. I was shivering, too, from the chill of the water and the dank air. Move, I thought, keep moving. There's got to be a way out.

I waded toward the far side. The stones were obscured by shadow, so that I couldn't see if there were any handholds or footholds that would let me climb up; the moss coating them had a sleek, ugly look, like the body of a slug. I remembered the flashlight. It was still in my pocket, but when I dragged it out and pressed the switch, nothing happened. Water had got inside the battery casing and made the thing useless.

I dropped it and began to ease along the stones to my left, searching for a foothold. There were a few knobs and projections like the one I'd braced my foot on earlier, but that was all. You couldn't climb up a vertical wall on little knobs and projections, for Christ's sake. A frigging mountaineer couldn't climb out of a stone well that way.

But I kept moving along the wall, pawing at it. My leg bumped against one of the bodies again; it seemed to bob away like a bundle of something heavy and discarded. Bundle. Two bundles, not one. Two stiffs in a well. Bundlestiffs. Bindlestiffs . . .

Cut it out!

I got a fresh grip on my control and hung on. I was going to get out of here, by God. I was going to find a way *out* of here.

And I found one—the length of two-by-two.

I was looking right at it, partially submerged with the upper end cocked against the stones in front of me. About five feet long, that piece of wood. The diameter of the well was no more than four feet. Twelve feet from the surface of the water to the wooden lip up there; three feet of water; fifteen feet overall from the bottom to the lip. And I was six feet tall, with a vertical reach of maybe three feet. Mathematics. Sure, that was the answer. Mathematics and that good heavy chunk of board.

I started to reach out for it. Then I thought: No, no, find a place to anchor it first. Again I groped sideways along the stones. I had to go half way around before I located a place—a moss-filled declivity formed by knobs on two stones laid atop each other, like a tiny recessed shelf, that was on a level with my wrists. I clawed at the moss, broke a nail and scraped my fingertips raw; but I got the indentation cleared out. By the feel of it, it was maybe a couple of inches wide and the same distance high—just about the size of the two-by-two.

The board was over on my right; I caught hold of it in both hands and slid it up at an angle against the opposite wall. Then I brought the bottom part over and pushed it into the slot between the two stones. It went in all right, stayed in without slipping. I wiggled the board until the other end looked to be resting at a point directly across from the slot, its length bisecting the well at an upward angle.

So far, so good. With my arms extended over my head, I waded out under the piece of wood until I could just touch it with my fingertips. Then I bent my knees, set myself, and jumped up and wrapped both hands around it and kicked my legs over against the facing wall. There was a tearing sensation in my left shoulder, an eruption of pain. But I managed to hang on, monkeylike, jouncing my body so my weight would pull the upper end of the board down tighter into the stones, wedge it there the way the lower end was wedged. I tried to keep most of the strain on my right hand and arm, but the left arm gave out anyway after four or five seconds and I had to let go. I kicked off the wall just in time, so that when I dropped my feet went straight down and I stayed upright and my head stayed out of that damned foul water.

Panting and shivering, I waded backward and reached up to test the two-by-two. The upper end was still a little loose; if I tried climbing onto it now, it was liable to slip and I'd have to do the whole thing over again. I could not afford to take that chance. The chill water was a constant drain on my strength, and there was that weakness in my left shoulder and arm. When I went up on that board it had to be one time only, one concentrated effort and no mistakes.

I stood for two or three minutes, massaging my left arm, going through some of the exercises the therapist had given me. The pain began to ease. I moved out under the two-by-two and jumped up again, using only my right hand; but that way I was only able to hang on for a second or two. I tried it again with the same results, but the third time I managed to stay suspended long enough to wrench downward violently on the top part of the board. When I waded back to test it this time it was wedged in tight between the walls: I couldn't move it at all.

I realized one of the corpses was lying against my leg and nudged it away. I could hear my teeth clacking together like old bones. The fingers on my left hand were stiffening up again from the cold. I needed that hand and arm—I could not make the climb otherwise—and I massaged them furiously from fingertips to armpit, exercised them, kept them out of the water. I did that for a good five minutes, not thinking about anything except getting out, getting out, feeling the sun on my body again.

Some of the cramping went away finally; I could flex the fingers almost enough to make a fist. I was as ready as I would ever be.

I squatted down until the water was just under my chin, so I could grope along the submerged part of the wall under the board's lower end. It had a slimy, repulsive feel. But some twelve inches below the surface I found a jutting corner that seemed large enough to use for a toehold. I rubbed at it, stripping away some of the slick growth to make it less slippery. Then I got the edge of my shoe braced on the jutting corner, reached up and took a two-handed grip on the two-by-two, dragged in a deep breath, and shoved and hauled myself upward, grunting with the effort.

The board seemed to move slightly under me. I felt the panic again—and then I was out of the water and draped over the wood with my right shoulder pressed against the wall. There was no more shift in the two-by-two—I might have imagined it—but I lay still anyway for a time. The strain on my left arm had turned it numb in places, as if parts of it were no longer attached; I wanted to rest a while before I had to use it again. But my abdomen was supporting all my weight and the two-by-two was cutting into it and making it difficult for me to breathe. I had to move right away.

I pushed back from the wall, turning my body so that my head was toward the stones and inching backward up the angle of the board. Still no shift in the length of wood; it *had* to be wedged in pretty tight. I kept moving until I was stretched out along it from crotch to chin, then slowly swung my left leg over. And eased myself into an upright position, straddling the board like a kid facing the wrong way on a narrow seesaw.

I sat like that, not moving, sweat leaking out of me, until my breathing returned to normal and little prickles of pain erased the numbness in my arm. The rough part was next: getting my feet under me, standing up on that slender two-inch expanse. I put my head back. The top of the well was only about eight feet away now; I could see the wooden lip, I could see more of the nearby trees and the fat gold underbelly of a cloud where the westering sun struck it. God, I thought, let me get *up* there.

All right. I inched forward again until my knees butted against the stones; felt down along the wall on both sides. No toeholds there. I leaned up and brushed my palms over the mossy rock higher up. Small projections here and there, precarious handholds at best, but I had no other choice. I dug the fingers of my right hand into one of them, braced my left hand on the board and my right shoulder against the wall, lifted my right leg and cocked the knee over the wood. Shoved up, pulled up, got my knee down on the board—and almost lost my balance. Frantically I clutched at the stones, throwing my weight against them. If the board had shifted then I would have come right off it and toppled back into the water. But it stayed wedged and I kept my perch, kneeling on the one leg with the other still hanging down.

My hands were slick with water and sweat, but I didn't dare let go of the wall or the board long enough to dry them. The strain was making my head ache so badly that I had difficulty keeping my thoughts together. And that was good because thinking led to mistakes in a situation like this. You had to act on reflex and instinct.

Balanced on the one knee, hands flattened against the wall, I turned my body so that I could bring the left leg up; put that knee down ahead of the other. Shifted my weight to the left leg, managed to draw the right one up far enough to get the sole of my shoe flat on the board. Crawled up the wall, pushing with the right foot, rising by inches. The muscles in the leg started to weaken, but by then I had the left shoe down too. Blank space of time, no more than a couple of seconds. And then I was standing up on the board, gasping, sobbing a little from the effort, belly and chest and the side of my face pressed against those cold, clammy stones.

When I stretched my arms upward my fingers slid over the wooden lip on top, a couple of inches beyond it. All I had to do now was grab hold of the lip and haul myself up and out. But my left arm was going numb again; I had to bring it back and down and let it hang loose at my side. Both legs had a jellied feel. I don't have enough strength, I thought. All this way, all this struggle, I can't pull myself the hell up there.

Then I thought: Goddamn you, yes you can. Yes you can! There's not going to be a *third* corpse in this frigging well.

The tingling came back into the left arm, and pretty soon a dull throbbing ache replaced the numbness. I concentrated on the arm, told myself I could feel strength seeping through the muscles and sinews. Made myself believe it. I already had my right hand hooked over the wooden lip; I brought the left up and made those crabbed fingers fasten around the lip too.

I shut my mind down, tensed, and lunged upward.

One of my flailing legs dislodged the two-by-two; I heard it skitter loose, fall and splash into the water. Pain ripped through my left shoulder and armpit, and the arm went numb again. I pulled frenziedly, my shoes scraping against the stones, not finding any purchase. For a moment I felt my grip on the wood slipping; then my right foot dug into a niche, held long enough for me to heave upward again and fling my right forearm over the lip. My head came up out of the well, and I saw the ground and the sun blazing through the trees, and somehow I got my left forearm over the lip too, and squirmed and struggled, and first my ribcage and then my belly slid over the upper ring of stones, over the curved wood . . .

And I was clear of the well, lying face down in the good sweet grass.

I was out.

I lay there for a time in a patch of sunlight, I don't know how long, waiting for it to warm me and some of the pain and tension to ebb out of my body. My mind felt sluggish, vague and dreamy. The last half-hour, all that had happened inside the well, seemed unreal, as if I had been given some kind of drug and had hallucinated the whole thing.

The police, I thought eventually, you got to talk to the police. And that made me stir, get up on my feet. The wind blowing across the clearing gave me a whiff of what I smelled like; it brought bile up into the back of my throat. I looked at the well, shuddered, and looked away again. My left arm flopped around like a hunk of sausage when I started to walk; I grabbed it in my right hand and pulled it in against my chest. It was starting to tingle again, to hurt, so maybe it would be all right.

I went around the front of the house, shambling a little, like a drunk on his way home from a wake. My car was still sitting where I'd left it. The rest of the clearing was deserted, or I thought it was until I got to the car and opened the driver's door. Because when I did that I glanced across at the near side of the house, and somebody was sitting on a small pile of lumber over there. Just sitting, not doing anything else. Not even moving.

The skin between my shoulder blades rippled. And my mind was clear and sharp again. I shut the car door, thinking: So this is the way it ends. She never left at all. She's been sitting here the whole time.

I understood why when I got to her. I understood a lot of things then, and all of them were ugly. Like murder. Like killing a sister.

Like Arleen Bradford herself.

23

She did not move as I approached. Just kept sitting there rigid and straight, hands flat on her thighs, legs crossed at the ankles, looking out over the valley. I stopped a couple of paces to one side of her. The sun was at my back, perched atop the distant crests of the Sonoma Mountains, and the way I stood put her in my shadow. But she still didn't seem to know I was there.

She was wearing an ankle-length skirt and a chaste white blouse and the kind of shoes mothers refer to as sensible. No makeup except for a little rouge on cheeks that were as white and thickly textured as gardenia blossoms. She looked all right until you saw her eyes. They were wide open and unblinking—not unlike those of Hannah Peterson's corpse down there in the well, and just about as lifeless. Pieces of dull glass, like windows behind which lay dark and empty rooms. The Arleen Bradford I had met four days ago, the prim and proper and caustic one, didn't live there anymore.

I moved over in front of her, so that I was blocking her view of the valley. That made her see me; she blinked once, but nothing happened in those vacant eyes except for a flicker of recognition. Her body held the same rigid posture.

"Oh," she said, "you got out of the well."

"Yeah. I got out of the well."

"Did you find Hannah? She's down there. Him, too. Lester Raymond."

"I found them."

"I knew you would when I saw you climb down inside."

"Is that why you tried to trap me in there?"

"Of course." There was no emotion in her voice; she understood what I said to her, she was rational and lucid, but something had short-circuited inside her. Or died inside her. It was like talking to a machine instead of a human being. "I didn't want to hurt anybody else, but I was afraid. I knew you would go to the police. I don't like to be locked up. Hannah locked me in a closet once when we were children. I hated that, I don't want to go to prison."

You won't go to prison, I thought. Not the kind of prison you mean.

I asked her, "Why are you still here? Why didn't you leave?"

"I don't know," she said. "I was going to. I was going to drive Hannah's car back to Sonoma and leave it somewhere. That's why I came all the way back here this afternoon. But then I would have had to do something with your car too. Drive to Sonoma twice, take taxis up here twice before I could go away again in my own car. It all seemed . . . I don't know, suddenly it all seemed too much bother. I've been sitting here thinking what I should do. But now that you're out of the well, it doesn't really matter, does it?"

"Where's your car now, Miss Bradford?"

"Down by the gate."

"Dark green, isn't it?"

"Yes. I left it there when I saw the gate open. I closed the gate yesterday when I left, so I knew someone was here. I walked up through the woods. I was very quiet; you didn't hear me."

"No, I didn't."

"They didn't hear me either. Hannah and him. I parked my car down by the gate yesterday, too, after I followed her here, and then walked up through the trees."

"You followed her from her house in Sonoma?"

"Yes."

"Why?"

"She was acting peculiarly. Red eyes, face all puffy—she hadn't been to bed all night. She wouldn't talk to me, after I drove all the way up from San Francisco to see her about funeral arrangements for Daddy. She was putting things in her car when I arrived—one of them was a rifle. But she was always afraid of guns. She told me to go away and leave her alone. I knew something was wrong. I always knew when something was wrong in Hannah's life. But I never imagined it was Lester Raymond. How could I have imagined a thing like that?"

"What did you do when you saw him?"

"I couldn't believe it. Hannah and Lester Raymond. That was monstrous enough, but then I overheard them talking. She was married to him once; he was the man she ran off with when she was eighteen, right after he murdered his wife. And now he'd murdered Daddy and she was helping him. She was *helping* him."

"Not by choice," I said. "He forced her to do it—

threatened to tell the police about their past relationship, probably."

That didn't seem to register. She said, "It made me sick to see them together, to know what they were. I've always hated her, you know. The pretty one, the favorite one. Daddy didn't care how much I loved him, he only cared about Hannah and himself. But it was as if she'd killed him too. You see? Her and Raymond, they killed my daddy. So I killed *them.* An eye for an eye. That's what the Bible says."

"How did you kill them?"

"With my gun. The twenty-two automatic I kept in my car for protection. Hannah was afraid of them, but I wasn't; I like guns. I'm a very good shot. I went and got it, and when I came back they were over on the other side of the house. Talking about a car—Hannah was going to buy a car for him. They didn't see me until I came up behind them. Then it was too late. I shot them. Him first, then Hannah. She screamed, the treacherous little bitch. It was a lovely sound."

I looked away from her, out over the vineyards and the villages and ranches that dotted the valley. There was a taste in my mouth like ashes.

"Then I dragged them over to the well and pushed them in," she said. "I don't look very strong, but I am."

I thought of the way she had jerked that ladder to pitch me off and then hauled it out. "Yeah," I said.

"I drove Hannah's car back into the woods and hid it behind the remains of an old building. I didn't think until this morning that I ought to take it back into Sonoma. If it was found abandoned up here, somebody might think to look in the well." She cocked her head to one side. "Why did you think to look in the well?"

"I'm a detective," I said. "I found the car, and I found some bloodstains in the grass where you shot them and where you dragged the bodies. They led straight to the well."

"Oh," she said. "Bloodstains. Yes. I should have thought of that, too. But there's so much to think of. I couldn't think of it all."

There's always too much to think of when you commit murder, I thought. And always something that you don't think of that trips you up. But it was pointless to say that to her. Her punishment had already started for her crimes, and it was far more profound than any society could mete out.

"What did you do with the gun, Miss Bradford?"

"It's down in the well. I put it in Lester Raymond's pocket before I pushed his body in. I didn't think I would need it anymore and I wanted to get rid of it; it seemed like the thing to do. If I'd still had it I would have shot you too. Instead of trying to trap you in the well. That would have made things much easier."

"Would it?"

She frowned in a confused way; it was her first facial expression since we'd been talking. "I don't know," she said. "I don't know."

I looked away again. There was not much else to say to her, or to find out from her; I had just about all of it now. All the major facts, anyway. I still didn't know much about what had happened on Friday night, but the only two people who could have told me were dead. Some of it I could guess at. Such as why Hannah had called me: an initial reaction to hearing from Raymond, a blind groping for help toward the detective who'd flushed her ex-husband in Oroville; but I hadn't been home, and when she'd had time to think it over she'd decided she couldn't talk to anybody, that she had to do what Raymond wanted her to in order to protect herself. And it seemed a good bet that she'd spent the night right inside her own house. Her bed hadn't been slept in because she hadn't gone to bed; she'd sat up, chain-smoking—all those cigarette butts I'd found in the fireplace—and in the morning, red-eyed and puffy-faced, she'd begun loading the rifle and other stuff into her car. The car had been in the garage all night; that was why she'd been loading it in there, instead of out in the driveway.

The rest of it, such as where Hannah had met Raymond on Friday night and what they'd said to each other and what plans Raymond had been making for his escape, had died with the two of them. As had the exact circumstances of Charles Bradford's death in Oroville. But those things weren't important. None of it was important, really, except that three people were dead—two of them, Bradford and his daughter, senselessly—and that a couple of old crimes and several interconnected new ones had not gone unpunished.

It seemed a hell of a price to pay for justice.

"What are you going to do now?" Arleen Bradford said. "Are you going to take me to the police?"

"Yes."

"I could fight you. You know I'm strong."

"But I'm stronger."

"Would you hit me?"

"If I had to."

"Then I won't fight you. I don't like to be hit. I don't like rough men."

"All right. Come on, then."

She got up, slowly, and smoothed her skirt, and we went over to my car. She said, "I won't be in jail very long. I can't stand to be locked up. I'll find a way to kill myself."

No you won't, I thought; there'll be doctors to see to that. I didn't say anything.

When she was inside the car I opened the trunk, stripped off my sodden clothes, and put on the change of old stuff I keep in there for fishing trips and unplanned overnight stops. It took me some time because of the weakened left arm. And because my head was pounding fiercely and making me a little dizzy.

On my way around to the driver's door, I glanced at the house—the house that might never be finished now. Bindlestiff Manor. And for some reason I had a sharp mental image of the hobo jungle up in Oroville, of the three old tramps and the way they'd come alive when the Medford freight rolled in. And I imagined I could hear the low cry of the locomotive's air horn, like a lament in the night that went on and on.

I got into the car. Arleen Bradford looked at me and said, as if she sensed what I was thinking, "Why did he have to disgrace himself by becoming a hobo? Everything would have been all right if he'd stayed in Los Angeles and found some kind of job. He'd have his inheritance now, he'd still be alive." She plucked at my arm. "Why did he do it?" she said. "Why did he have to die?"

Every man on his grave stands he, and each man's grave is his own affair. And each woman's, too.

I started the car and drove us away from there.

24

I did not tell the authorities about the time I'd spent in the well. Arleen Bradford didn't tell them about it either; she was badly frightened at the prospect of being locked up, and for the most part that was what she kept babbling about. I still smelled a little funny, even with the change of clothes, but none of the county cops and neither of the two FBI agents who showed up later bothered to ask me about it.

There were a couple of reasons I left out the part about the well. One was that I didn't want it to get into the newspapers. And it would have; it was just the kind of macabre thing reporters and city editors love to exploit, and they'd have splashed it all over the front pages of the *Chronicle* and the *Examiner* and half a dozen other tabloids in the Bay Area, complete with photographs. I had had enough of that sort of sensational publicity; I couldn't afford any more, especially not now. The stuff that would get into the papers about me finding the bodies and bringing Arleen Bradford in was bad enough, considering that my position with the State Board of Licenses was still pretty shaky.

The second reason I didn't mention the well incident was Harry Runquist. I was the one who called to tell him what had happened. The cops wouldn't do it right away because he wasn't Hannah's next of kin; and as much as I hated the job, it would have been cruel to let him go on sitting and waiting beside the phone. He took it the way I knew he would, unraveling a little at the edges; I was glad I could not see his face just then. If it came out about the well, all the grisly details of me being trapped in there with the two bodies, it would have been that much worse for him. I did not want to be cruel that way either.

On the drive back home that night I decided I was not going to tell anybody what I'd been through up there. It was an experience I wanted to start forgetting, and that meant not talking about it. There would be dreams—there were always dreams after ugly incidents like this one—but they would stop after a while. The memory would fade and blend with all the other memories after a while, too. And only come back now and then, like an old twinge of pain or a malaria chill.

So when Kerry showed up after work on Monday

night, over her snit at me and bubbling with questions, I told her everything that had happened in the Valley of the Moon but I didn't tell her about being in the well. She noticed that my left hand was still pretty cramped up, but I told her it was because of what had happened on the freight train in Oroville. The upshot of the omission and the little white lie was that she didn't start lecturing me again. And she didn't try to make me dwell on the case, either, which was fine with me.

"Have you heard any more from the State Board?" she asked.

"No."

"That's a good sign, isn't it?"

It was and I said so. We were sitting in the kitchen, Kerry with a cup of coffee and me with a can of Schlitz. She looked wonderful in a black skirt with a gold chain belt and an emerald-green blouse. I looked like a slob because I'd just finished taking a shower when she got there and I was still in my old chenille bathrobe, the one she'd been after me for weeks to get rid of; she said it looked like something mice had been nesting in.

She asked, "Have you talked to Eberhardt?"

"No. Not since Saturday."

"How did it go then?"

I gave her a capsule account of the conversation I'd had with him.

"Sounds grim," she said. "Have you made up your mind yet about the partnership?"

"No. I will pretty soon, though. Pretty soon."

She was silent for a couple of seconds. Then she gave me an up-from-under look, one of those shrewd jobs of hers. "What about your Chinese girlfriend?" she said. "Did you talk to her today?"

"Ah, Kerry, come on. There's nothing between Jeanne Emerson and me."

"But she'd like there to be."

"That's ridiculous."

"Is it?"

"Sure it is," I said. And it ought to have been, but I was afraid it wasn't. Jeanne Emerson *had* called again today, while I'd been downtown letting the FBI ask me a bunch more bright questions, and left a message saying she'd like to get together some night this week. To talk about the article, she'd said, but she'd also suggested we have dinner. I hadn't called her back. Yet.

Kerry said, "Are you going to see her again?"

"How do you mean, 'see her'?"

"Are you going to do that article with her?"

"I don't know, maybe."

"What if she tries to seduce you?"

"Hah."

"But what if she does? What would you do?"

"Fight her off with a whip and a chair." But the question made me feel uncomfortable. "Listen," I said seriously, "don't be jealous, okay? I was jealous of you and look where that got us; we almost broke up over it. I don't want that to happen again."

"What makes you think I'm jealous?"

"Well, you've been acting jealous . . ."

She reached over and picked a piece of lint or something off the sleeve of my bathrobe. Then she winked at me. "For a detective, you make a lot of wrong deductions. That's because you're too literal-minded."

"What's that supposed to mean?"

"Don't be too sure I was as jealous as I seemed on Saturday," she said. "Maybe I just wanted you to think I was jealous."

"Oh, so that's it. What were you doing, testing me?"

She shrugged. "Figure it out, detective," she said and winked at me again.

I gave her a long speculative look. Then I said, "So what do you want to do?"

That caught *her* off balance. "About what? Dinner, you mean?"

"We can worry about dinner later. I was thinking about now, the next couple of hours."

"I don't know," she said. "What do you want to do?"

"Practice my salesmanship, for starters."

"Salesmanship?"

"In case I ever lose my license again and wind up having to take a job as a clerk in a men's store." I stood and leered down at her. "Would you care to see something in a bathrobe, madam?"

"My goodness! Such as what, sir?"

I took her into the bedroom and showed her.